Braced

Scholastic Inc.

Arthur A. Levine Books hardcover edition designed by Abby Dening, published by Arthur A. Levine Books, an imprint of Scholastic Inc., April 2017.

ISBN 978-0-545-90761-3

10 9 8 7 6 5 4 3 2 1   18 19 20 21 22

Printed in the U.S.A. 40
This edition first printing 2018

Book design by Abby Dening

For Mom and Dad

one

I'M ON THE FIELD in my navy-and-white uniform, tapping my cleats lightly on top of the ball in front of me—*right, left, right, left.* The air smells like just-cut grass and brand-new rubbery soccer balls, and I've got that pre-game feeling: happy and sick to my stomach and laughing so hard my muscles hurt, all at the same time.

I'm in the back row next to Hazel, and Frannie is up front with Ladan leading the warm-up, because they're the captains for this scrimmage, which also means they're both definitely starting. No surprise there. They're the best players on our team. Frannie, Hazel, and I are best friends, but we're usually split up during soccer, because Frannie plays forward, and Hazel and I play defense.

Ladan leans over and whispers something to Frannie. Her shiny black hair falls over her shoulder in a never-ending ponytail. The whole time Frannie and Ladan are talking and tapping, it's like they aren't even thinking about what their feet are doing.

"Toe taps to the right," Ladan shouts.

I follow her lead, running in place, moving the ball between my feet like I've been practicing with Frannie all summer. Then I slide the ball with the sole of my shoe, turn, and keep tapping, staying in sync with the rest of the team. I love the way it sounds when everyone moves together.

"Great work," Coach Howard says. "Let's take a quick water break, and then we'll huddle up."

We all jog over to the bench. Frannie and I both chug from our water bottles. Hazel applies another layer of sunblock to her peachy skin. Coach Howard is standing at the other end of the bench, scribbling on her clipboard.

I know I shouldn't sit, in case she calls my name, but I'm getting nauseous standing here waiting to find out if I'm starting. I never have before.

Today is our first scrimmage. It's my chance to prove I'm ready to start and maybe even play forward this year, and I have to leave at halftime to see the doctor. Mom waited until last night to tell me about it. She said she couldn't change the appointment, because Dr. Paul's schedule gets booked up months in advance and going to see him is more important than soccer in her opinion, which means I have to make every second of the first half count.

"All right. Come on over," Coach Howard says.

Everyone huddles around her. I stand at the edge of the circle, because I feel like I might puke. Hazel grabs my hand. "Fingers crossed for you," she whispers.

"For you too," I whisper back and hold on tight.

"As far as I'm concerned, this is the most important game you'll play all year," Coach Howard says. "I want you to get out there today and give it your all. Stay focused. Work together. Work hard. Hydrate. It's hot out here. If you don't hear your name right now, that means you'll be playing a bigger role later in the scrimmage. But everyone will be on the field today." Hazel and I look at each other and smile. "We'll start with the forwards: Ladan on the right, Frannie center, and Saaya left."

I feel my heart speed up. I need to stop freaking out for no reason. It's not like there was a chance I was going to start on offense, since I don't even play offense.

"Midfielders: Lauren on the right, Zeva and Emily in the middle, and Katrina on the left." *Breathe.* "Now, defense." Coach Howard stares at her clipboard like she can't read her own handwriting, or maybe she's changing her mind about who she thinks should start. "Brianna in goal," she reads off the page. "Let's go with Josie on the right. Hazel left." I squeeze Hazel's hand. She squeezes back harder. There's only one more spot.

"And last but not least—" Coach Howard's eyes travel

around the circle of girls like she's searching for someone. They land on me. "Rachel, I'd like you in the middle."

"Really?" I cover my mouth as soon as the word spills out. I hear someone giggle.

"Really," she says.

Yes! Yes! Yes! This is happening: I'm starting in the first scrimmage of the year.

"Let's get out there and win," Coach Howard says. "Hands in."

Everyone reaches into the middle of the circle. "GO BULLDOGS!" we shout as loud as we can.

We win the coin toss, and I jog out onto the field.

The ref blows the whistle, and Ladan kicks off, passing to Frannie. She dribbles down the field, and our offense owns the ball for most of the first half. No one scores, but it feels like the whole game is happening somewhere far away, on the other end of the field. Even though no one on defense has touched the ball, Coach Howard swaps Hazel out for Angela right before the end of the half, which doesn't seem fair. I smile at Hazel and cross my fingers. I hope I don't get taken out before I have a chance to do something.

Ladan and Frannie swerve through green jerseys, passing the ball back and forth, landing where the other person needs them to be at the exact right moment. It's like they're in on a secret.

There are only a few minutes until the end of the half. A girl in green steals the ball away from Lauren outside the penalty box. She dribbles around Emily and Zeva and heads straight toward me. Before I can think or talk myself out of it, I'm running to get the ball from her. The green jersey tries to fake me out with a high wave, but I don't veer to the left like she wants me to. Her feet aren't fast enough to move around me, and I drag the ball away from her. I look for someone to pass to. No one is open, and no one is coming after me yet, so I dribble down the field.

That's when I realize I'm not sure if I'm actually allowed to do this. I'm supposed to be manning the goal, but this is my chance to prove I can play offense. It might never happen again. I keep dribbling. Out of nowhere, one of their players is in front of me. I drag the ball back and then pull it forward, going around her. Frannie is open on my right, and I pass to her. She shoots it straight into the net.

The whole team erupts, cheering and screaming, as the ref blows his whistle three times, signaling the end of the half. Frannie runs over and grabs me. "Rachel!" she shrieks, jumping up and down and pulling me with her. "We scored!"

Hazel runs up behind us. "You got an assist!" she screams, hugging me and pulling Frannie in. I hug them back. The whole team crowds around us, jumping and chanting, "BULLDOGS, BULLDOGS, BULLDOGS, BULLDOGS."

It's like nothing I've ever felt before. It's sunshine and whipped cream and someone calling you their best friend for the first time, only better. I feel like I'm floating.

"Brooks," Coach Howard calls.

I jog over to her. She's standing by our bench holding her clipboard. She played forward in college, and she has her nose pierced, which I think is cool. She changes the ring almost every day. Today it's a blue, shimmery stud that looks pretty against her dark brown skin. "Way to hustle out there, Rachel. You're playing like a real champ." She pats me on the back.

"Thanks, Coach."

"We all wish you could be here for the second half. It's too bad you have to leave."

"I really want to stay." I feel my heart in my throat.

"This is a one-time thing, right?" she asks.

"Right," I say quickly. "Definitely." My next appointment with Dr. Paul won't be for another six or seven months, and I'll make Mom schedule a morning appointment, so it's a one-time thing for Coach Howard.

"Then we'll see you at the next practice," she says.

"I'll be there the whole time," I say.

"Okay. Good." She looks down at her clipboard.

Most of the team is standing around our bench drinking water and eating orange slices. I walk past them and over to

Hazel, who's off to the side juggling a ball. She looks up at me without letting it drop. "Time to go?" she asks.

"Yeah," I say. "Unfortunately."

"Ugh. I hate the doctor."

"Seriously." I act like I'm just going to some regular checkup that's totally normal. I've never talked to Hazel or Frannie or anyone other than Mom and Dad about going to see Dr. Paul. I guess I don't really like to think about getting monitored.

"Why couldn't your mom just change the appointment?" she asks.

"No clue." I shrug. "Bring home the win," I say to her.

"It'll be a lot harder without you," she says. "But I'm on it!"

I smile and jog off the field before she has a chance to ask me anything else.

A few hours later, Mom and I are in Boston at the hospital, waiting for one of the x-ray techs to call my name. I watch the same cartoons that have been playing on a loop since we got here and lean against the wall, stretching out my hamstrings. I need to stay loose for soccer. I close my eyes and try to pretend I'm anywhere else. Only it's impossible to ignore the smell, like cafeteria green beans and cabbage. I can tell Mom is trying not to breathe it in by the way her white linen scarf is wrapped tightly around her neck and nose. She rubs her swollen stomach. She's pregnant. It's weird. Hazel and Frannie totally agree with me. I mean, we're in seventh grade. No one else's mom is having a baby.

"I think it smells worse today," I say to Mom.

"I thought it was just me." She points to her belly. She doesn't have morning sickness, exactly, but she told me everything smells stronger and more disgusting thanks to the baby. "I have another scarf," she says. "Want it?"

"Yes, please," I say.

She reaches into her bag and pulls out a blue-green floral-print scarf.

I sit down next to her, cover my face with fabric, and breathe in a mix of detergent and Mom's sweet perfume. "Much better," I say, because it actually helps a lot. "Thank you."

"Good. I'm glad," she says. "So, who won your scrimmage?"

"I don't know yet." I shrug. "I missed the second half, remember? And no one has texted me back."

"I'm sorry, honey. I know you're disappointed." She pats my knee. "But there was nothing I could do."

"Except change the appointment," I say.

"We have to make sure your back is okay. This appointment is important."

"Soccer is important to me," I say. "This scrimmage was a really big deal."

"I know, and I'm sorry I had to pull you out, but you're lucky to be seeing Dr. Paul. He's the best pediatric orthopedic surgeon in the country."

I already know how great Dr. Paul is, and I don't feel like talking about him. No matter what Mom says, I don't think it's fair that his schedule is more important than everyone else's. "I got an assist," I say. "My first one."

"That's amazing. I'm proud of you for making the most out of the time you had."

"Thanks. I did, and I promised Coach Howard this would never happen again, so it can't, okay?"

"Rachel—" She sighs.

"Brooks, Rachel," a woman in pink scrubs announces.

Mom stays in the waiting room while I disappear behind the double doors. This is the easiest part of the day, because I'm the only one in the room when the machine is taking pictures of me.

The x-ray tech opens the door to a small, empty room. "Please change out of your clothes and into a gown. Leave your underwear on, but remove your bra," she recites, without making eye contact.

I close the door behind her and change, thankful there is a stack of gowns on the shelf so I can take two—one to cover me in front and one to wear like a bathrobe. I can't think of anything worse than walking through the halls with my underwear sticking out for the whole hospital to see. Well, I can, but I'm not going to think about what's coming next.

After they're finished taking my x-rays, Mom and I go back to the main waiting room for another hour before my name is called again, and we're taken into this little white room that smells like rubbing alcohol and latex gloves. The woman who called my name takes my height and weight, and then we wait more. My phone buzzes. It's a group text from Hazel: We won!

YES! I write back. What was the score?

One-nil, she says. You assisted on the only goal!

It would have been one-one, if Hazel hadn't headed the ball off the goal line, Frannie adds. She totally saved us from drawing.

That's amazing! I say.

The doorknob turns. I sink further into the sticky vinyl chair. I act like I'm too busy texting Hazel and Frannie about the scrimmage to notice the doctors, but really I'm counting their shoes—four pairs of oxfords and three pairs of identical clogs. I hate odd numbers and teaching hospitals and surgeons, except for Dad.

"Rachel, can you say hello to Dr. Paul?" Mom says in this high-pitched, singsong voice, like it's my first day of preschool and she's introducing me to everyone. It's stupid, because I obviously know Dr. Paul. I've been coming to see him twice a year since I turned eight.

"Hi," I say without looking up. I'm not trying to give him attitude or whatever it is Mom thinks I'm doing. It's just that I know what's coming next, and looking up will make it worse.

“How are things with David?” Dr. Paul says to Mom.

“He’s doing well. Very busy.” She doesn’t remind Dr. Paul to say hi to *me*.

“Busy is good. I’m glad to hear it. I think we’ve all been working a lot more this month since we had to take off for the Orthopedic Association meeting.”

“Absolutely.” She grins. “David said your keynote was very interesting.”

“That is too kind.” I try not to roll my eyes. “Please send him my regards. I’m sorry we didn’t have a chance to catch up at the meeting.”

“I will. Of course,” she says, all excited and on the edge of her seat. Mom and Dad both act like Dr. Paul is some huge deal because he went to Harvard and now he’s a famous spine surgeon, and one time his picture was on the cover of this magazine about the best doctors in Boston. I don’t care about any of that.

But it’s not worth kicking the chair against the wall or running out of the room or telling Mom I want a different doctor. I’ve tried every escape plan. They all get me back here, to this same place, to this little white room.

“What do you say we have a look at that back of yours?” Dr. Paul says to me. His voice sounds robotic, with a trace of a British accent.

I stand up and walk as slowly as I can across the room. I don’t look up at the doctors. I stop walking when I see the shoes in front of my bare feet, five-ish steps away. I turn my back to the shoes and wait.

Mom tucks her golden hair behind her ears and stares at Dr. Paul like he has all the answers. She takes a deep breath. She's so focused on making sure my spine is okay that sometimes it seems like she forgets I'm here.

Dr. Paul unties the back of my gown.

I squeeze my eyes shut and hold my breath.

"Bend forward and let your arms hang in front of you like you're trying to touch your toes," he says.

I bend forward, but I don't let my arms fall between my legs like Dr. Paul wants me to. I clench the gown with my armpits. I can't let it fall. The last time I saw Dr. Paul—six months ago—I was shorter and completely flat. Today I'm wearing purple boy shorts, which is lucky, but there's no way I'm going to stand in front of all these doctors in nothing but my underwear.

My stomach rumbles.

"Hungry?" one of them asks.

Shut up.

Dr. Paul places the measuring thing against my back. I feel the gown slip a little and hang around my shoulders. I force the fabric to stay where it is. He moves the device down my back, holding it against me so I can't move, and all the blood is rushing to my head. "The patient was last seen on April seventh, and in that time she's grown four and a half inches.

She has a family history of scoliosis. Her mother had a spinal fusion at age twelve," he says to his residents, who are like apprentice doctors. "I'm going to use the Scoliometer, to do what?"

"Determine the rotation in the patient's spine," one of the female residents says.

"Good," he says. "What else am I looking for?"

It will be over soon, as soon as he measures my spine and checks my x-rays and says the number. Then we can get in the car and go home and pretend this never happened for another six or seven months.

"Distortion in the torso," another resident says.

Nothing I do or say is going to change the truth about why I'm here: I have progressive idiopathic scoliosis. Translation: My spine is curving into an "S" shape. The funny thing about scoliosis is that my back feels normal, like anyone else's, but I guess that part is only temporary. If the curve keeps getting worse and doesn't get treated, it can be really painful and change the shape of my ribs and eventually make it hard for my lungs and heart to work the right way. I guess it's a lot harder to fix the curve after I'm done growing, which is why I'm being monitored now.

"Go ahead and stand up," Dr. Paul says to me.

I cover myself with my gown and sit next to Mom.

Dr. Paul walks over to the computer monitor by the door and pulls up two x-rays of my spine—one from my last visit and one from today. He measures the angle between the top and bottom of the curve in my spine to determine the degree of my scoliosis. That number is how I'm being judged. Dr. Paul is checking to see if the curve in my spine is bigger, because as I grow, it's sort of hard for the curve to get smaller by itself. That happens for some people, but I haven't been that lucky so far.

"Thirty degrees," Dr. Paul says, turning away from the screen.

I was twenty before, so the number is higher than last time. It's higher by *a lot.*

I look at Mom. She's looking at Dr. Paul and biting down on her lip.

"I was hoping we wouldn't get here, Amy. I'm sorry." His words are softer and less like an automated message when he talks to Mom. "With your family history and a thirty-degree curvature of her spine . . ." I hate how he's talking about me like I'm not even here. Like I don't count. "I don't think we have a choice. We have to brace her."

"Okay," she says, but there are tears in her eyes, and it doesn't seem okay.

"What's going on?" I ask.

"The curve in your spine has progressed," Dr. Paul says, looking at me for once. "I'm recommending that we treat your scoliosis with a back brace."

"A what? No. Mom, I don't want a back brace." I look at her.

"I know you don't, sweetheart." She rests her hand on my

shoulder, rubbing in slow, gentle circles. "I wish this wasn't happening. But if Dr. Paul says you need a brace, then you do. We have to do everything we can right now to stop your curve from getting worse. This is your chance to avoid surgery."

I look at Dr. Paul. He's looking at his phone.

"But you had surgery and you're fine," I say.

"I was really lucky, Rachel. There are big risks when you have a spinal fusion. The surgeons use metal rods and screws to straighten and fuse the vertebrae into a solid bone. You don't want surgery unless you absolutely need it." She grabs my hand and looks at me. Her eyes are welling up again. "I love you. And we're going to do everything we can to make sure that doesn't happen."

I nod. I didn't know any of that about her surgery. "What does a back brace even look like?" I ask.

Mom takes a deep breath. "It goes under your clothes, you know, like the brace I had on my knee, only this one is plastic and there's padding on the inside that helps keep your spine straight as you grow." Mom hurt herself running last spring, and she had to wear a brace for a few weeks. You couldn't see it under her pants.

"They should have samples in the brace shop," Dr. Paul says, like he thinks that's helpful.

"It'll be okay. I promise," Mom says. "It's not nearly as bad as what I went through. You're lucky. Trust me."

"Okay," I say. "I do."

~

When we get home, I go straight up to my room and turn on "Soccer Jams," aka the greatest compilation of pump-up music ever. I'm really into making playlists, and I'm not trying to brag, but this one is a masterpiece. I turn it up until it's loud enough that I can't hear myself think about getting a back brace or about how much longer it's going to be before Dad gets home from work—but not *so* loud that I get in trouble. I need Dad to be here now to answer the most important question ever: Can I still play soccer after I get a brace?

I didn't think of it right away because Mom said the brace was like hers, and she could still run with the one she had. But then when we were walking out to the car, I realized that sometimes when people get braces or casts, they have to sit out of sports. By that point, it was too late to ask anyone other than Mom, who said she wasn't sure and I should ask Dad. I thought about calling him on the ride home, but today is an operating day, so his phone is off and there's no way to know what time he'll be home.

I let the happy, fast-paced songs find their way into my head. One by one they pick me up, until I'm dancing in circles on the soft carpet, moving around my room to the beat. When the garage door rumbles open, I realize I forgot I was waiting for it—for Dad.

I run down the stairs and into the kitchen. Dad is standing by the stove whispering something to Mom. She stirs a big pan of vegetables with one hand and rubs her stomach with the other. She nods quickly and a lot of times but doesn't say anything back to him.

"Hi, Dad," I say.

He smiles and walks over to me, hugging me with one arm. He's still holding his briefcase. "I know this stinks, kiddo. But we're going to get you better. I promise."

"Okay. But Dad, I really want to play soccer so badly."

"Did Dr. Paul say you couldn't?" he asks.

I shake my head. "He didn't say anything about sports, but I didn't tell him I play."

"I can't think of a reason why you'd have to stop playing soccer altogether. You need to ask when you go back. But I really don't think it's going to be a problem."

"See? Look at that!" Mom says. "And if you had surgery, you'd be out for at least six months, maybe even a year. This is so much better."

I look at Dad.

He nods. "It's going to be okay."

two

THE NEXT DAY, Mom and I are in the brace shop at the hospital. I change into the gowns and sit down, trying not to fidget. There's a loud sawing noise on the other side of the door, and the air smells like melted plastic.

A tall woman wearing a white coat and a name tag that says "Julie Olson, Orthotist" walks into our room. "You must be Rachel," she says, pulling up a small swivel chair and sitting down directly across from me. "I'm Jules." She smiles at me with all her teeth. "Today is going to be quick and easy. I'll take your measurements and a scan of your torso. Then we can talk more about your brace. You'll come back in a week for a fitting and we'll start easing you into the brace."

"That's great," Mom says.

Jules smiles at her, adjusts her glasses, and then looks at me.

"Can we talk about the brace first and then do all the other stuff?" I ask her.

"Of course. We can definitely do that."

"Okay, good, because I really want to know if I can still play soccer after I get the brace. I'm starting now and I might play forward soon. And I'm not giving that up."

"That's great," Jules says. "We want you to stay as active as possible." I hold my breath, waiting for her to answer my question. "We use your scoliosis to determine your treatment plan. Every patient's scoliosis is slightly different, which means each plan is different." She opens my chart and scans the information. "Dr. Paul has prescribed your brace for twenty-three hours per day."

I'm not sure I hear her right. No one said I'd have to wear it all day, even to school and while I'm sleeping. I look at Mom, but she nods her head like a puppet.

"I can't wear a back brace all day," I say.

"Yes, you can," Mom says. "You have to, honey."

"But soccer practice is an hour and a half."

"Some patients are able to take an extra hour or so out of the brace for sports, but it depends on your situation." Jules looks at Mom when she says that part. "Dr. Paul recommends that you don't take your brace off for more than an hour, because of your family history and the quick progression of your curve, combined with the projected length of time between now and when you're done growing."

"If Dr. Paul is not recommending it, we're not doing it," Mom says.

"That's not fair! What I am supposed to do?" I look at Mom. "You said I wasn't going to have to quit."

Mom looks at Jules.

"You could practice for half the time," Jules says. "You'll want to save an extra fifteen minutes every day to shower and stretch. It's important to keep your skin clean."

"That's like being half on the team. So no." I sound as mad as I am.

"The other option is you can try playing in the brace. You'll need to let your parents know how it's going in terms of balance and comfort. And you'll need to protect your skin—it can get itchy inside the brace. But at the after-school level, I'm comfortable with you giving it a try as long as you're careful."

"There you go." Mom says it like it's that easy. "That's a great option."

"Okay," I say, because it's not like I have a choice.

Mom adds, "This is your chance to get that new ski jacket you've been asking me for. I mean, your old coat won't fit over the brace. It was getting too small anyway. You've grown so much this year."

"That doesn't make sense—I'll be out of the brace by winter." Dad never keeps his patients in casts for more than a few months.

"I don't know, honey." She sighs.

I can feel more bad news coming, like the dark, heavy air that moves in right before a thunderstorm. "How can you not know?"

"It depends on when you finish growing. If you wear the brace now, your spine will be forced to grow straight. I'm not sure how long that will take."

I look at Jules. "Your mom's right," she says. "Most people stop growing about two years after they get their first period, so for you that's another six months. Maybe closer to a year."

"A year—" My voice cracks. *No.* This can't be happening.

"It goes by fast," Jules says. "Really—it isn't so bad."

It feels horrible.

Jules walks across the room, opens a drawer, and takes out what looks like a stretchy tank top. "If you could put this on, we'll get started," she says.

I stand up and my stomach drops fast, like the time I rode the flume at Canobie Lake Park with Dad. Only Dad isn't here to hold my hand and make it better. I wish he'd taken part of the day off and come with us. But I've known for a long time, that even if Dad says yes to an event, it doesn't mean he's definitely going to be there.

I untie one of my hospital gowns and let it fall onto the floor. I'm not sure if Mom came up with the idea of two robes or if Gram used to get her two. Mom hardly ever talks about what it was like when *she* had surgery for scoliosis, and she always makes it sound like someone else's life or some faraway world that has nothing to do with her now. I untie the other gown and hold it over the front of my body while I slide the tank top over my head. I pull the stretchy fabric down as far as it will go.

One upside to the cast room: I get to keep my bra on.

"Stand as tall as you can with your arms by your sides and your chin up," Jules says to me. "I'm going to take measurements like I'm fitting you for a dress."

I follow her instructions. She measures across my chest and shoulders, and then around my ribs, waist, hips, and the very top of my thighs. She pauses after she takes each measurement and writes the numbers down on a form.

"Okay, here comes the fun part." She picks up what looks like a wand with a camera on the end. "I'm going to use this scanner to capture a digital image of your torso. You won't feel a thing. All I need you to do is put your arms out to the side in a T shape, then bend your elbows, and do your best to stand still." She walks in a circle all the way around me, holding the scanner out in front of her and moving it up and down and around. "You're all done," she finally says to me.

"That's it?" Mom asks.

"For today," she says.

I change back into my clothes and sit down next to Mom.

"Do you have any other questions for me?" Jules asks.

"Yes," I say. "I want to know what the brace looks like."

"I can show you a sample. I have one in here." She smiles at me, then walks across the room and opens up a big cabinet by the door. "Before I take the brace out, I want to mention that this is for someone a bit younger than you, so it's—colorful. And your brace will have a different shape than this one since we're going to make it specifically for your scoliosis. But you can at least start to get a sense of it."

She takes out a hard plastic—*thing*—and brings it over to me. It's like a stiff tube top, with curved edges on the top and bottom, and a seam in the back. It reminds me of a turtle shell, only it goes all the way around. It's purple with a yellow-and-pink design, and even though it's meant for a much smaller person than I am, the plastic and padding are a lot bigger and thicker than I expect.

"There are lots of designs—all different colors and characters," Jules says. "I can show you the options now if you'd like."

I shake my head. "I want a plain one."

She nods. "Good choice. That way you won't have to worry about seeing the color through your clothes."

"Why does it look like that?" I ask. "I mean, it's so thick."

"I'll show you." She pulls apart the plastic edges of the seam so I can see inside the brace. "The straps are missing, but as you can see, the brace opens in the back. A thin cushion on all sides protects your skin, and then pads placed in specific areas push on your spine to keep it straight as you grow. The brace won't necessarily fix your scoliosis, but in most cases it will stop the curve from getting worse."

I know I'm looking right at a back brace, but it's still bright and small and hard to imagine what mine will be like. Or maybe I don't want to picture it, because now that I know I have to wear it to school and soccer, I'm afraid the brace might not be okay.

A week later, we're back at the hospital. We had to wait until the afternoon to come here, because Mom had a doctor's appointment in the morning to make sure everything was all right with the baby.

There's a knock and the door opens. "Rachel, Amy, good to see you both again," Jules says. "Rachel, I'd like you to put this on." She hands me a different stretchy tank top. "It's sort of like an undershirt for your brace. You'll want to wear one of these all the time to protect your skin."

"From what?" I ask.

"The padding will rub against you at first. It takes some time for your skin to toughen up and adjust to the brace, but it will. Try not to use lotions or anything scented on your stomach."

I nod.

"So, are you ready to see your brace?" she asks, like she's a game show host.

"Do I have a choice?" I say.

"No," Mom cuts in.

"Go ahead and change, and I'll be back in a few minutes."

Jules leaves and I put on the white stretchy undershirt. It has thin straps and goes all the way down below my underwear, like a really short, tight, spaghetti-strap dress. It's kind of cute, only there's a weird little flap under my left armpit. I tuck the extra material inside the shirt, like it's a tag that shouldn't be sticking out, because it seems like a mistake.

I don't say anything to Mom or sit down. I'm too nervous.

Finally, the door opens, and Jules is standing there holding my brace. "It was made just for you," she says, like that's a good thing. Only I'm looking right at it, so I know it's definitely not.

The brace is so much bigger than the sample she showed me. It's huge and thick and bright white, and the holes scattered across the torso make it look like a machine. I can tell right away that it isn't meant for just my back. On the left side, it goes up to my armpit and dips far down below my underwear, covering part of my thigh. It's longer in the back than in the front, like it has a built-in tail. Fake plastic hips on both sides stick way out. I don't even have real hips yet. On the back, three Velcro straps as thick as my forearm rattle their metal clasps every time Jules moves. It's going to make me look wide and weird, like I swallowed a bathtub.

Jules hands it to me. It's heavier than I expect, and I need both hands to hold it. It slips out of my fingers and crashes to the floor.

"Rachel," Mom says. "You need to take care of your brace. It's important."

"I didn't mean to," I say. "I'm sorry."

She shakes her head.

"Why don't we give it a try?" Jules asks, picking the brace up off the floor.

I bite down on my lip and do my best not to look directly at it. *It's going to be fine. It has to be. It'll probably look better once it's on.*

"Rachel, I'd like you to take a deep breath and suck all the way in."

I breathe and squeeze my stomach. She pulls open the back of the brace and wraps it around me. The top unfinished edge scrapes the skin under my armpit. It burns as the brace settles onto my hips. Jules grabs the extra flap of material from the tank top and pulls it over the part of the brace that goes into my armpit.

There is an inch of heavy plastic and padding all the way around my torso and ribs. It cuts under my bra, pushing my chest up and out. On the left side, where the brace goes into my armpit, a pad digs into my back, and on the right, another one presses against my ribs. The brace is squeezing my waist and rubbing my hips, forcing me into a straight line.

I can feel the tank top riding up my leg and over my underwear. I reach for the bottom of the tank to pull it back down, but the brace is in my way. I can't bend enough to cover myself.

"I need you to take one more deep breath," Jules says. "And I have to warn you, this part might be slightly uncomfortable."

It gets worse?

She tugs on the bottom strap in back, and the brace clamps down on my hips and butt. She shuts the top strap, and it crushes my ribs. I can tell she's pulling as hard as she can when she shuts the middle strap because she accidentally grunts a little, like it's hurting her.

I'm fighting to find air in my lungs. I cough and gag, like I'm choking on food. There isn't enough space for me in here. "I think it's too tight," I say.

"You just need to get used to it," Mom says.

It feels like I'm getting punched every time I breathe. "It really hurts."

"You're fine," she says. I keep waiting for her to say, "We'll figure it out, Rachel," like she would if we were anywhere else, talking about anything other than this, but she doesn't say anything.

"It's going to take some getting used to," Jules says. "I know that seems impossible right now. That's what all my patients say at first. But don't worry. We'll ease you into the brace, a few hours at a time, and eventually you won't even notice it's there. I promise."

There's no way anyone could get used to this. She should try wearing it. She'd hate it.

"We'll have you start with an hour today, while you're here in the hospital. Then you'll add a second hour tomorrow. After that, I'd like you to follow the schedule I've created for you until you're wearing it twenty-three hours a day." She holds up a piece of paper. "In a few weeks you'll come back, and we'll take some x-rays to make sure the brace is the right fit."

"I can't even move," I say. "There's no way I'll be able to run."

"It will take time to adjust," Jules says. "But it shouldn't be a problem."

"We'll go shopping this week," Mom says. "You'll need new—"

"Everything," I finish her sentence.

"Try to be positive, Rachel." Mom shakes her head. "It's just plastic. It's not permanent. You should be thankful you have a brace. This is your chance to avoid surgery. You're lucky."

"I don't feel lucky."

"Well, you are."

The pads inside the brace feel like sharp rocks being pushed against my ribs and back, and the middle of my body aches already from being crushed on all sides. And it's not getting any easier to breathe. I reach around for the strap, and the brace pinches my skin. I ignore it. The top strap is right there, but I can't get my hand all the way around it. The Velcro is fresh from the package, and it won't budge. I twist my arm as far as it will go, until it feels like it might pop out of the socket, but it's not getting me anywhere. I'm stuck.

"What are you doing?" Mom asks.

"It hurts. It really hurts."

"Oh, honey," she says. "You have to stay in it for an hour now. Give it a chance."

"Mom. Please."

She doesn't say anything, again.

I'm trapped.

three

USUALLY AS SOON as we leave the hospital things go back to normal, but with the brace rattling in the backseat, it's like we took the hospital with us. Mom doesn't say a word to me the entire drive. It should take only a half hour to get from Boston to Andover, but thanks to traffic, we've been in the car for at least twice that long by the time we get to our exit. Mom taps her fingernails against the steering wheel the whole way.

"Should we get Sal's?" she asks, breaking the silence.

I shrug. "Pizza is fine," I say.

"Pizza is your favorite food."

"I can't believe you said it was like your knee brace," I say. "It's huge. I'm not wearing it. I can't. It hurts."

"You have to. You don't have a choice," she says. "And you

can't cut corners on your time in the brace. This is serious. You could end up permanently deformed. Do you understand that?"

"Yes," I say. I *am* scared of what will happen if my curve keeps getting worse. I don't want to be hunched over or in pain or anything else. I want Dr. Paul to be able to fix me. I just don't want to wear the brace.

She turns the car onto our street and parks in front of the mailbox. "Go inside and rest. It's been a long day. I'll pick up a pizza and those garlic knots you love." She tucks my hair behind my ears. "Any other requests?"

I get that takeout is her way of trying to make it better. "No, thank you." I shake my head and open the car door.

"Rachel." Mom stops me. "We'll go shopping this weekend and get you a bigger soccer bag that will fit the brace."

"Do you really think I'm going to be able to play soccer?" I ask.

"I highly doubt Jules would tell you that you could try if it wasn't possible."

"Okay." I hope she's right.

I walk up the driveway and straight into the backyard. I check to make sure no one is watching before I open the hidden door under the deck, crouch a little, and disappear inside. Mom and Dad never think to look for me in the storage space, so it feels like my secret place.

I sit down on my pink beanbag chair and kick my feet up onto the stack of firewood. It's been there for a few years, ever since we first moved into this place—Dad's dream house. At the time, he thought he'd be home enough to build a real fire occasionally. Now the old stacks of wood remind me how much I hate the hospital, and how it seems like Dad loves it more than everything else.

My eyes cloud with tears. I don't bother wiping them away. I take a deep breath, letting my nose fill with fresh pine and mulch. I cry until I feel my phone buzzing in my pocket. It's a text from Frannie: Hazel and I are going to dinner at Tortillas with the forwards. Coming?

Normally seeing Hazel and Frannie would automatically make everything a billion times better. And this is basically my dream: hang out with my best friends, talk about soccer, and eat burritos. But there's no way I can fake happy and act like everything is fine right now. I have this sinking feeling in my stomach, like the brace is going to get in the way of everything I want.

Here's the truth: I call Frannie my best friend, but I have no clue how to talk to her about my brace. Frannie is super confident and basically never does anything embarrassing, and sometimes that makes me feel like she's inspecting my insides with a magnifying glass, judging me every time I mess up. So she doesn't know about that one time last year when I got my period in the middle of math, or that I keep deodorant in my backpack because I'm afraid I'll forget to put it on one morning and have bad B.O. all day. Whenever I tell her a little too much, I end up feeling stupid and saying, "That's not what I meant," even if I've said exactly what I meant. And that's just how I feel when I tell her small things. I've never had to tell her about anything big until now.

It's different with Hazel. She totally gets me. She never says "TMI" or "That's weird" like Frannie does, because she knows what it's like to feel super awkward, and to worry about what other people think. I always feel like I can tell her anything. Except right now, I don't know how I'm supposed to tell her about this.

I text Frannie back. Food poisoning ☹.

OMG! What about practice??? You can't miss it, she writes back.

I'll be there! Nothing is going to stop me, I say.

Okay. Phew. See you at 11:30 tomorrow!

☺☺☺

Two seconds later, I get a text from Hazel: You okay?

Feeling WAY better, I say.

K cool. Just checking ☺. We miss you!!! I'm still coming over before practice, right?

Totes! I say.

I feel bad for lying to them. We aren't the kind of friends who keep secrets, but once I say it out loud, scoliosis won't be this thing that only exists with Mom at the hospital. It will be part of me every day. And the brace won't be over until I'm done growing. Whenever that is.

four

WHEN I GET downstairs the next morning, the kitchen is empty. I make my signature breakfast—cereals mixed together—and pull myself up onto the counter while I wait for the milk to soak in. I pick up one of the mason jars next to me and twist off the top. It's filled with the seashells Mom and I collected at the start of summer. Inside, it smells perfect, like sand and salt water, like that day at the beach.

I can hear Mom talking on the phone. She's in the bathroom down the hall with the door closed and the sink running. I guess I'm supposed to think she's washing her hands in there, but I keep hearing her say my name. It's probably Gram or Dad on the other end of the phone, but I still wish she'd stop talking about me, because it feels like she's opening the door to the little white appointment room and letting everyone look inside. I bet she'd hate it if I did that to her. I should get to tell people about the brace first.

She turns off the faucet. "It'll be fine. Really. It will be," she says, even though she has no clue how it's going to be. She doesn't have to start seventh grade in a back brace. "Have a good day, honey," she says, so now I know for sure she's talking to Dad. I walk over to the bathroom and knock on the door.

"David, hold on a second—" Mom says. "Come in."

"Is that Dad?" I ask, swinging the door open.

"Rachel wants to talk to you," Mom says into the phone. "Okay. Love you too." Then she hands me the phone.

I turn my head away from her. I'm not talking to her right now, and I want to make that very, very clear.

She sighs and walks out.

"Hi, Dad," I say. "The brace hurts."

"It's supposed to be like that at first. It takes time to break it in," he says. "It will get easier."

"Okay. But when do you think that will happen, because I can't move in it right now. And I really want to be good at soccer still."

"Then you will be. You can do anything," he says. "Just don't forget to have fun. Give yourself a break from thinking about all this stuff. It's important."

"Okay," I say.

"I love you," Dad says.

"I love you too." I hang up and walk into the kitchen. I ignore Mom and look down at my bowl of cereal. It's exactly the way I like it, a little mushy. I take a bite. It's sweet, sugary perfection.

Mom walks over to the fridge, and the silver charms dangling from her bracelet clap together, like tiny bells celebrating her every move. She opens the door. *Ring.* Takes out the yogurt. *Ring. Ring.* Slices cantaloupe. *Ring. Ring.* She eats the same breakfast every day, same as me.

"Rachel," she says, turning to look at me. "You have to wear *it* for two hours today. I don't want you to tell me later that you already forgot about your new responsibility."

I can't forget. I can't think about anything else. How does she not get that?

"Okay?" she asks.

"Okay." I realize it's sort of impossible to ignore Mom when I need her to put the brace on me and take it off. "Can you help me with it?"

"Now?" she asks.

"Yes. Now." Hazel is coming over today so we can hang out before practice. I'm not ready to tell her about the brace, which means I have to get into it now so I can be out of it before she gets here. The thought of putting the brace on with anything in my stomach makes me queasy, so I dump my cereal in the sink and put my bowl in the dishwasher.

"You have to eat something," Mom says.

"I will when I'm done wearing it."

She doesn't fight me. I go upstairs and change into the tank top Jules gave me at the hospital. It's way less cute in the real world.

Mom walks into my room holding a sweatshirt and looks around like she's searching for something. Last summer, I finally got rid of all the shiny bows and stuffed animals that were clogging up my shelves. Mom let me pick out a new comforter and curtains. The colors are cranberry, cream, and dusty blue. I think it's cute and put together, with my own personal antique-y style, but not trying too hard. Just like me, or what I want to be. I don't have cutouts from magazines taped to the walls like Hazel, but there's a besties collage on my desk and a stack of journals hidden under the bed.

Mom gasps when she sees the brace where I left it yesterday: on the floor in a pile of laundry. "You don't just throw it on the ground, Rachel. You're lucky to have a brace."

I wish she'd stop saying that.

She leans forward and picks it up. Her spine doesn't bend when she reaches down. It stays straight and fused together, because of her surgery. I never really noticed that she leans in a straight line before. It's part of her, one of the things that has been there forever, like the thick white scar along her spine, and the way she says certain words with a Boston accent and smells like home.

"Ready?" she asks, as if I have a choice. I don't, so I walk over to her. "It's easier to put it on if you start with your arms straight up in the air," she says. "That way it won't scratch your skin. It'll rub during the day no matter what we do, but at least we can avoid it first thing in the morning."

"How do you know that?" I ask.

"I wore a brace before my surgery. For . . . I'm not sure how long." She pauses like she's thinking. "I know I got it in sixth grade, because I went to a new school that year."

"You don't remember?" I ask.

Mom shakes her head. I can tell she's trying to find the answer hidden deep down in the basement of her brain. "Six months. Maybe nine. It was a long time ago."

"If you had a brace, then why did you need surgery?" I ask.

"Bracing doesn't work for everyone. I don't know why it didn't work for me. I followed all the rules, but my curve kept getting bigger. The next time I saw the doctor, it was fifty degrees and I needed surgery."

My chest feels tight. "Were you scared?"

"Yes." Her eyes turn red and glossy. "Come on, let's get you into the brace," she says.

I follow Mom's advice and lift my arms up. She takes a deep breath and wraps the plastic around me, resting her hand against my back. She pulls each of the straps shut as quickly as she can—bottom, top, middle. It still clamps down, but it doesn't scrape or sting this time. It's a lot less painful than when Jules did it.

"After you take it off, if you have any blisters, you have to put rubbing alcohol on them," she says. "It will help your skin toughen up. It stings, but it works, and I don't want you to have scars. I'll leave some under the bathroom sink. The rubbing alcohol is Gram's trick. Did I tell you that already?"

I shake my head.

"I could have sworn I did. Well, anyway, it's worth it. Believe me. I don't have one mark." She pauses. "From the brace."

"Okay. I can do that," I say, and I mean it. I don't want any permanent marks either.

"Good." She smiles. "I almost forgot—" She hands me the sweatshirt. "I figured you'd need something to wear around the house."

I pull it over my head and slide my arms through the soft sleeves. It's warm against my neck, and it smells like fabric softener. I've never seen Dad wear it before, but I know it's his, because it hangs down past the brace and touches the tops of my knees. I turn on an old homework playlist, get in bed with my book, and cover myself with a blanket, disappearing under the thick fabric.

"I'm going downstairs to rest for a little while. Call if you need anything." Mom sits down next to me and kisses my forehead. She holds on to my face, pressing her cheek against mine. It feels soft and warm and nice not to be alone. She gets up and walks to the other side of the room, then turns back around to look at me. "I know it hurts, but you'll be used to it soon," she says. "Just follow the rules."

Two hours later, it's finally time to take the brace off. Mom doesn't come up to my room, so I get out of bed and go to the top of the staircase. I put my left foot out in front of me and bend my knee like I'm about to start walking, but I can't find my balance and I can't move my hips. Not one at a time. They have to go together.

I hold the banister and lean back. It feels like I'm stuck inside a sweaty rain boot. Every time I step down, the brace digs into my sides, and all I can think about is how impossible and far away playing soccer feels. I force myself to keep going until I make it to the bottom of the stairs.

Mom isn't in the kitchen, and Hazel will be here in five minutes. She's always on time. It's one of the things I usually love about her, but today I wish she'd show up late.

I can't move at my normal pace without feeling like I'm suffocating, so I do the only thing I can think of: I take a deep breath and scream, "Mom!"

My cry for help bounces off the ceiling and right back at me. I wait for her to say, "In here, Rachel," but the house is silent.

I walk through the family room and into her bedroom on the first floor. Sometimes she can't hear me if she's taking a bath or curled up in bed. But Mom isn't in her room or in the tub or outside on the back porch. I'm on my way to check the kitchen again when I see her out the window. She's at the end of the driveway, talking to Hazel's mom, leaning into the driver's side window of the car. What is she doing? She knows I can't get out of the brace on my own.

I hear the back door close and the sound of flip-flops clapping against the floor. "Rachel!" Hazel says.

I bolt into the bathroom. "Be right there," I shout, slamming the door shut and tearing off my sweatshirt in one desperate move. I only have a few minutes before she'll come looking for me. *If I can get out of this thing and shove it under the sink, everything will be fine.* I twist myself around and grab the strap, digging my fingernails into the Velcro. I ignore the sharp pain under my arm and pull as hard as I can.

"Tell me you aren't still sick," Hazel says at the exact moment I feel the strap slip out from between my fingers. She's on the other side of the door, snapping her gum. "This practice is going to be huge for you. Frannie thinks Coach Howard might try you at forward. There's no way I'm letting you miss it."

"I'm not sick," I say, wiping my hands on one of Mom's fancy, embroidered towels. "I just woke up late."

"That's so un-you," she says.

I feel bad for lying again, but I can't exactly talk about this right now, and even if I could, I don't want to.

"What are you doing in there anyway?" she asks.

"I'll be out in a sec." This is the part where I'm supposed to open the door and be like, "Oh, hey, hi. What's up?" Only I can't. "We have Snapple in the fridge," I say.

"Cool." Hazel drags out the word so it's obvious she thinks I'm acting weird. "I'll get them for both of us."

"Thanks," I say. I reach back around and pull on the strap as hard as I can. My heart is pounding and my neck is sweating, the way it does when I wear my puffy coat in the car and the heat is on full blast. The strap doesn't budge. This can't be happening. I can't be stuck. Not now.

"Rachel," Hazel says. She must have taken off her flip-flops because I didn't hear her this time, and before I have a chance to come up with another excuse, the door swings open and she's standing there.

"What's *that*?" she asks, pointing at me.

I look at the ground and count the tiles, hoping to disappear. Hazel starts to giggle. It's soft and jittery at first and then it gets louder. I know it's her nervous habit when she feels awkward or embarrassed about something, but that doesn't make it hurt less. If this is how my best friend is reacting to my brace, I don't want to know what everyone else is going to do and say.

Before I realize what's happening, I'm crying.

Hazel immediately stops laughing. "What did I miss?" she asks.

"I can't get out," I say. "I need help."

She nods like she's glad there's something she can actually do. I turn around so my back is facing her and accidentally look in the mirror. Plastic has swallowed the middle of my body. I look a lot worse next to someone normal.

"Uh, what do I do?" Hazel says. She's looking at the brace like she's afraid to touch it, like if she's not careful, it might swallow her too.

"The Velcro," I say. "Can you undo it?" My words barely make it out.

Hazel pulls the straps open and I push the plastic apart, twisting myself until I'm free. I shove the brace under the sink and put my sweatshirt back on.

"I lied about being sick," I say. "I'm sorry—"

She shakes her head.

I nod, because I know what she means—that it's okay. Hazel and I are the kind of friends who are more like sisters. I don't have to apologize for faking sick when something is actually wrong.

"I have to wear it every day."

"But not to school," she says.

"All day," I say.

"What? That's so not okay." She sounds mad. "Did you get hurt or something? You were totally fine at the scrimmage. I don't get it."

"Nothing happened," I say. "I have scoliosis, and I guess it got worse."

"Is that why you had all those random doctor's appointments?"

"Yeah." I try to remember what I told her. I know it wasn't much.

"I was wondering what that was about."

"My spine is curving, and they're trying to keep it straight." I take a few tissues and blow my nose. "My mom had the same thing. Only worse. She had this surgery where they put a metal rod along her spine." It's a lot easier to feel bad for Mom when she's not in the room.

"Wait! What? That's super serious. You're not having surgery, right?" Her forehead crinkles up and her eyebrows squeeze together. "Are you?"

"I wish I were." I feel like a bad person as soon as the words come out of my mouth. It's not true. Not really. I know surgery is hard and scary in a different, bigger way. But then I wouldn't have to wear a brace to school and people wouldn't be weirded out by me. They'd be worried.

"How long do you have to wear it?" she asks.

"I don't know. . . . At least six months, maybe a year."

The words linger in the air like a thick cloud of smoke, making it hard to breathe. "It feels like forever."

Hazel opens her mouth to say something and then doesn't. She sighs, and it feels like she's taking back whatever she was thinking. I wish she'd tell me what she was about to say before she stopped herself. Hazel has this way of making everything bad seem like it's not that big of a deal, and all of a sudden, I'm afraid this is *so* big that nothing will make it better.

"I have no idea how I'm supposed to play soccer in this thing," I say.

"There's no way. You can't play in that."

"They said I could."

"Oh. Wow," she says. "Are you sure you want to?"

Yes, I think. Only I'm scared that if I say that, Hazel will tell me I'll never be good now, and I should quit. And then I won't be on the team, and we won't be friends in the same way anymore, and I'll be left out of everything. "I love soccer," I say.

"Okay. Then we'll have to figure it out. We will. That's just what's going to happen." She smiles at me.

I smile back. This is exactly what I needed to hear. "Promise you won't tell anyone. Not even Frannie. I really want to tell her myself."

"Promise," she says. I know she means it. "I'm glad you told me."

"Me too," I say.

"I'll get snacks. You get ready for practice." She points her finger at me. "You can't show up looking like you've been crying. You can trust me to tell you the truth. That's what besties are for."

It feels good to hear her call me her best friend right now, like somehow it means more than it did before she knew about the brace. "Get a lot of snacks," I say. "I'm so hungry."

"Ditto!" Hazel smiles again.

I leave the brace under the sink, next to the toilet paper and cleaning supplies, and change into my number-one favorite practice outfit: a blue tank top with a built-in sports bra and multicolored soccer shorts. I wash my bright-red eyes, so no one can tell I was ever upset, and dab a little cover-up on my new chin zit. I take a minute to look in the mirror and smile at myself. I'm ready.

When I get downstairs, Hazel and our moms are standing in the kitchen. "Did you get something to eat?" Mom asks me.

"I'm about to," I say. The fact that she was supposed to help me out of the brace either isn't registering or doesn't matter to her. She doesn't care that the brace hurts or that I can't get out of it on my own or that I wasn't ready to tell Hazel. The only thing she cares about is that I follow all of Dr. Paul's stupid rules.

"All right. I should get going." Hazel's mom hugs her. "Have fun, girls!" She gives me a half smile and a sigh. Hazel and her mom have the same orange tint in their hair and the same facial expressions. Neither of them is very good at hiding what they're thinking. She's looking at me with sad, scrunched-together eyebrows, like she feels really bad, which means Mom must have told her about my brace. I wish *my* mom would feel bad for me.

"Aloha!" Frannie walks in wearing a mini grass skirt over pink soccer shorts. There are leis around her neck and wrists and she's carrying a huge bag with more grass skirts and other tropical accessories. It's tradition to dress up for at least one pre-season practice, and costumes are sort of Frannie's thing. She drops her bags and kisses me on both cheeks. Frannie has been doing the whole kiss-kiss French thing since she got home from Paris in July. Last year, after she went to India, she was all about henna and chicken tikka masala.

Hazel can't stand it. She winces when it's her turn for the double kiss. And the second Frannie looks away to adjust the flower tucked into one side of her sandy blonde hair, Hazel rolls her eyes so hard I think they might fall backward into her head. I wonder if she ever rolls her eyes at the things I do.

Frannie hands both of us grass skirts.

"This is perfect." I smile and try to let the happy Hawaiian vibe soak in.

"I don't know. It might be kind of weird," Hazel says.

"Just put it on," Frannie says.

"But if we get made fun of . . ."

"We won't."

"There are going to be other people at school. It's not just the girls' soccer team."

"Stop." Frannie sounds annoyed.

"Okay. Fine." Hazel gives in. The two of them disagree the most out of the three of us, because Frannie is all about trying new things and Hazel usually wants to do what everyone else is doing. I fit somewhere in the middle, but probably closer to Hazel.

"Where did you get all this stuff?" I ask.

"Lucy took me shopping before she left for school." Frannie puffs out her chest a little, like her big sister is a movie star, which she probably could be if she liked acting instead of the violin. "She left me a ginormous pile of clothes too. She only wears black now that she's a hard-core musician."

"You're so lucky," Hazel says.

"Yeah, I know." Frannie smiles with her mouth closed. I can tell she's trying not to let herself think about anything except her new wardrobe. Ever since their mom died two years ago, her sister is always away at boarding school or Habitat for Humanity or summer programs for overachieving violinists. I don't blame Frannie for wanting to live in a make-believe world of double kisses and grass skirts. Sometimes it's easier to pretend to be someone else, especially when who you really are makes you sad.

"It's not fair. I'm done being the oldest. I'm abdicating," Hazel says. "I don't get anything good from my brothers."

"Oh, shut up," I say. "Don't even talk to me."

We all laugh. It helps when I turn the whole Mom-being-pregnant thing into a joke.

"I'm thinking we should work these into our Halloween costumes," Frannie says, pointing to her grass skirt. "We could get the whole team in on it."

"Yes!" Hazel says. "I want to be something really cute this year."

I close my eyes because I feel like I'm going to puke. I can't think about October or dressing up with the team.

I should tell Frannie about the brace now, because I'm going to need her help figuring out how to play soccer in it. But I know she'll say I have to tell Coach Howard today, and I'm not doing that. I get that it's selfish to practice with the forwards when everything is about to change, and when someone else could be practicing on offense instead of me. But I only have a few more chances to play without the brace, and I want to use them to prove I'm someone who matters to the team.

An hour later, the three of us show up to practice in our grass skirts and leis. Everyone rummages through the clothes and accessories that Frannie brought. Ladan adds a yellow flower to her shiny black hair. She's wearing a gray vintage tee that's worn in and fitted at the same time. It says "من فارسی صحبت می کنم" on front, with the English translation on back: "(I speak Farsi.)" I always think I look semi-cool until I'm standing near Ladan, and then it's obvious I'm trying way, way too hard. "I heart these grass skirts," she says to Frannie, wrapping a short one around her waist. Ladan is the most popular girl in our grade, so if she thinks something is cool, it is.

That's when the boys' soccer team walks across the field. Tate is in the back with Kyle. He looks even cuter than last year, if that's possible. He's tan and his hair is a little floppy in the back. And all I can think about is the bus last year: how he'd slide into the seat next to me, and we'd talk the whole way home.

I don't realize I'm staring at him until he looks right at me with his clear blue eyes. He smiles, and my heart starts pounding so fast I almost forget to breathe. I look away as quickly as I can, because no one can know about my crush, especially not Tate.

"Let's circle up," Coach Howard says. "As you can all see, we're sharing the field with the boys' team today. I don't want that to distract from our practice. We have a big game the first week of school. Let's get ready for it. Pair off and take the next ten minutes to work on passing."

Hazel and I don't have to say anything. We're always partners. I grab a ball and dribble down the field and over to her. I pass the ball to Hazel with the inside of my right foot, aka my weak side, trying to control where it lands, like I've been practicing.

"Don't think I didn't see what happened with you and Tate." Hazel stops the ball and then taps it back to me. "You totally had a moment."

I don't want to say anything that might jinx it, so I shrug and smile and pass the ball back.

"What if he asks you out? That could happen," she says. "I mean, we're in seventh grade. Guys are going to ask girls out all the time. It's not some once-in-a-lifetime thing like last year."

I hadn't thought about it like that. "Do you really think he would ask me out?"

"Seriously?" Hazel rolls her eyes. "Stop fishing."

"I'm not," I say. "Wait, am I? Because I didn't mean to do that."

Hazel smiles. "I'm kidding—about the fishing part. Not about Tate. I mean, think about it—anything could happen. Especially now that you're a superstar soccer player."

"Shut up," I say, chipping the ball into the air.

Hazel bounces it off her chest and shoots it back to me.

We pass back and forth until Coach Howard claps to get everyone's attention and we all circle up again. "We'll be divided up by position today. I want you to work on developing the skills you need to master your role on the team. For example, the forwards will be running drills that focus on speed, ball control, and footwork." She's holding her clipboard and the special piece of paper that says where everyone belongs. She puts her hand on Frannie's shoulder. "Forward," she says and then moves on to the next person.

I hold my breath. Coach Howard circles me a few times, naming the other offensive players, before she comes back around and puts her hand on my shoulder. "Forward," she says.

I smile so big it hurts. Coach Howard thinks I can do it. She's giving me a chance to prove that what she saw in the scrimmage is real.

When the team breaks up, Frannie takes off her leis and waves them around over my head. "I knew it!"

"Thanks," I say to her, then I look at Hazel. "Are you good?" I ask her, because if I'm playing forward, she's going to be alone on defense.

"Totally," she says.

"Because, I mean, you're my best friend, and if you—"

"Rachel." She stops me. "I'm good."

"Okay," I say.

"We're still passing partners, right?"

"Um, for life." I smile at her.

"Good." She smiles back. "You're ready for this."

It feels good to have Hazel and Frannie on my side.

All of the forwards, including me, stand in a small circle and stretch. "Hey," Ladan says. I'm not 100 percent sure she's talking to me, since it doesn't happen that often, but I look at her in case. "You're good this year."

"If you're saying it, it must be true," I answer.

"I always forget how funny you are, Rachel Brooks." She says my name like I'm a character from a TV show she sort of likes. "I think it's chill that you're playing forward today."

"Thanks," I say. "Me too!"

We put our feet together and reach for the ground. Ladan folds herself in half like she's about to do something where yoga is involved. It's funny how cool people are always naturally flexible and good at things like yoga. I can hardly touch my toes.

We start with a four-corner speed dribble, which sounds easy, except the other girls are all so fast. I try to focus on my inside cuts and not pay attention to what everyone else is doing, but it's hard to ignore Ladan running right behind me like she wants to push me out of the way. It's better when we switch directions, because my left inside cuts are stronger than almost everyone else's, except for Frannie's.

"Very nice footwork, Rachel," Coach Howard says. I don't look up. I stay focused. I can do this. I know I can.

We set up for one-on-one shooting drills. I'm up against

Saaya. I dribble forward and drag the ball right. She lunges, and I pull the ball left and kick it into the goal. *YES!*

I score three more times. By the time I have to go up against Ladan, I feel good, and I think I could maybe play forward in a real game situation.

Ladan is tough from the start. She stays on me, and no matter what I do, I can't get around her. She's quicker than I am—fact. She keeps sticking her foot out, trying to get the ball away from me. I can't let that happen. Finally, I fake left. She goes for it, thinking I'm trying to set up my shot. Instead I drag the ball back, switch feet, and shoot with my right, before she has a chance to block. It hits the goalpost and bounces back at me.

Coach Howard blows the whistle. "Nice work, everyone," she shouts.

We all head over to the sidelines.

"That was awesome." Frannie gives me a high five.

I shake my head. "That last round—"

"You went for it. That means something. Trust me."

I nod.

"I'm telling you the truth," Frannie says.

"I know." I smile at her. "Thank you."

"Hey, Rachel," Ladan says. "Welcome to the offense."

I wish I could freeze this moment and everything could stay exactly the same.

Tate is standing next to our bench. “Offense, huh?” he says to me. “Way to go, bus buddy,” he adds, like that’s a thing we call each other.

I smile. He’s so cute. That word doesn’t even do him justice. “Yeah, I had an assist in the scrimmage, so—”

“I heard,” he says. “Impressive.”

He heard? I play with the end of my ponytail, because Hazel told me that boys like it when you do that. But he isn’t looking, so I do it again to make sure he saw.

“Big Tate Dog,” Kyle shouts. “Let’s split.”

“In a few,” Tate says back.

“Seriously, bro. That’s weak.”

“Whatever,” Tate says.

Kyle walks over to Hazel, and I hear her giggle. She’s in love with Kyle Montgomery, even though lately she’s been all, “Kyle who?” I know she’s just afraid of what will happen if she admits how she feels and then finds out he doesn’t feel the same way. I’m afraid of that exact same thing.

There’s a sort of weird silence. It reminds me how nervous I am.

“Give me the summer highlights,” Tate says.

“My mom’s pregnant.” *UGH. Why would I ever say that? Seriously. What is wrong with me?* I can feel my stupid words hanging in the air between us.

“That’s awesome.” He smiles at me with both dimples.

"I wish I had a little bro or a sister. That would be cool. Do you know which one it is yet?"

"No clue. But yeah, a brother could be cool." I hadn't thought about the possibility that it could be a boy. I just assumed it would be a girl. "Your turn. What's going on with you? How's Adam?"

He shrugs. "He left for college last week." One day when Kyle tried to get Tate to ditch gym and then made fun of him for not doing it, we started talking about how his older brother, Adam, kept getting in trouble for skipping school. After that, we talked about Adam all the time. Tate said once that I was the only one he ever talked to about him. "I mean, it's really good for him. Not so great for me. I already miss him."

"I'm sorry," I say. I want to tell him that I get what it feels like to miss someone, because Dad is gone most of the time, but I can't figure out how to say it. Then Kyle shouts, "Tate-O," so I just look into Tate's eyes and nod.

"Let's do it, dude." Kyle aims his water bottle at Tate and it accidentally squirts Ladan.

"Stop being annoying," she says. Then she squirts him back with her water bottle.

"Bring it on," Kyle says. She rolls her eyes and turns away.

"I should go," Tate says.

"If you, um, ever want to talk more about your brother, I can listen."

"That's really cool of you to offer," Tate says. Then he walks over to Kyle.

When I look up, Ladan and Hazel are both smiling at me, like maybe they can tell this is a thing—Tate and me—and not just in my head. Maybe Tate asking me out could be a real possibility, except everything is about to change.

five

MOM SIGHS WHEN she realizes we have to park in the red garage at the mall because the blue lot is full. There's nothing *that* wrong with the red garage, but it means we got a late start, and somehow the day already feels ruined.

She swerves through tight rows of parked cars until she finds an empty spot and pulls in. I get out and open the trunk. Every time I move, I feel this blister on my hip where the brace tugged at my skin too hard. Mom told me not to scratch or pick at it unless I want it to be there forever, and I don't, so I tuck my free hand in my pocket and try to think about anything other than scratching. The trunk is empty except for my brace, which is hidden in a pink cloth bag I found in the downstairs closet. The swirly Pepto-colored pattern is all happy and attention grabbing, which I don't want, but it was the only thing I could find that was big enough to carry the brace. I drape Dad's sweatshirt over the top so the plastic ends don't peek out.

"Let's go," Mom says.

I slam the door shut, and we walk through the parking garage toward the elevators.

"Where should we go first?" she asks me.

I shrug and let her question hang in the air. Sad truth: I haven't spent a single second thinking about my first-day-of-school look since the brace happened.

Mom and I ride the elevator up into the mall. When the doors open, she turns right as if she's heading straight for Macy's. I can't stand the thought of walking into a big department store. "Maybe we should try Olivia's," I say. I might have more room to breathe in a small boutique.

"Great idea." Mom taps her nails lightly against my back.

Olivia's is the kind of place where they only have one or two of everything, so it all looks extra special and one of a kind. "Let me hold your bag," Mom says to me as soon as we walk in. "You need both hands to shop."

I hand her the pink bag and smile, because it's the kind of thing Mom would say if everything were normal. But then she slings it over her shoulder and the sweatshirt falls off, landing on the floor. She picks it up and drapes it over her arm. The ugly plastic ends of my brace are sticking out for everyone to see. I keep waiting for her to realize what's happening and cover it up, but she doesn't.

"I'll just carry it," I say.

"What's the problem?" Mom asks.

"I don't want it hanging out like that!"

"Fine." She shakes her head, then shoves the bag into my arms and walks away so I know it's *not* fine. I cover the brace before anyone else has a chance to see it and follow her toward one of the salespeople.

"Hi, Justine," Mom says, glancing down at the girl's name tag. "I'm looking for clothing options for my daughter. She has to wear a brace for her back, and she's a little embarrassed about it." Mom says it like she thinks she's whispering, but really the entire store can hear her.

Justine nods and looks over at me. She's wearing a fitted dress covered in sunflowers that hugs her tiny body. She's all perky and happy to help. I hate her for thinking she understands me. "I'm guessing Rachel wears a size four."

"Except she'll need to go up a few sizes." Mom says that part a little softer than before.

The lump in my throat is growing from a small marble to a rock, and the tears in my eyes make everything blurry. This isn't exactly news. I get why I need new clothes; I heard Mom say this before on the phone with Gram. But I don't want to go up a size, or a few of them, because once the evidence is hanging in my closet, the brace will be real.

"Can I see what we're working with?" Justine asks, walking over to me.

"Of course," Mom says, following her. I hold on to the brace as tight as I can. I feel like a genius for taking it away from Mom. She'd probably whip it out in the middle of the store if she had the chance.

"Not right here," I say.

"Oh. Sure." Justine has this sweet, soft voice that people probably compliment her on. "Tell me, Rachel, what's your style like?"

"I don't know." I shrug. "I don't have one." It's a blatant lie. Hazel says certain things look like me: retro patterns, lace details, and soft, happy colors. I have a feeling my style is another thing that's going to change this year. "I want to blend in," I say.

Justine nods, trying to figure out what to do next. "What do you think of this?" She picks up a slouchy, glittery sweater I'd never wear.

"Um, no," I say.

"It's really cute on. It looks totally different."

I shake my head. I hate when people say that. It's usually a lie, and I don't care how this sweater looks when it's on. I'd never wear it, ever.

"Come on, Rachel," Mom says. I can't believe she's taking Justine's side.

"Why don't I pull some options and bring them into the fitting room for you?" Justine asks.

"That'd be great," Mom answers for me.

I'm pretty sure I see Justine roll her eyes at one of her co-workers when she thinks we aren't looking.

The fitting rooms only have curtains for dividers and doors. Anyone can peek through the leftover space between the wall and the fabric. "I don't like this kind of dressing room," I say. The way the curtains sort of tie together, but never really close, reminds me of hospital gowns.

"Me neither," Mom says, sitting down on a chair inside one of the rooms.

I ignore my phone vibrating in my pocket. Frannie's been texting me all day about sleeping over after practice tomorrow. I can't. I have to wear the brace for *eight hours* tomorrow, and right now, soccer is the one thing that feels good and regular. I'm not going to tell Frannie and ruin that until I absolutely have to.

There's a mirror on the back wall, which means I don't have to go anywhere to see how I look. "I'm nervous everything is going to look bad," I say to Mom. I want her to tell me it's not true, to say, "We'll find something. We'll figure it out."

"I thought you wanted to come to this store," she says.

"I didn't want to go to a department store."

"Oh," she says.

"I like my old clothes."

"They're not going to fit. And you can't wear that sweatshirt to school for the rest of the year."

"Why not? Maybe I will." I know I'm making it worse, but everything Mom says feels like the opposite of what I need.

"Fine." Mom sighs and rubs her belly, like talking to me is taking up too much energy, and she has more important things to worry about, like the baby.

Justine walks in a few minutes later with shirts, sweaters, and pants draped over her arms. There's so much hanging off her she looks like she might topple over.

"Thank you, Justine," Mom says. "We appreciate your help."

"No problem. I'm going to leave everything in here. Let me know if you need me to pull any other sizes for you."

"Thanks," I say.

She smiles at me and walks away.

Mom takes my brace out of the bag and holds it up in the air like it's a prize. After she's done tightening the Velcro straps on me, she picks up a blue shift dress with little flowers. "This is cute. Don't you think?"

"Yeah. Maybe." I nod. "It could be."

She hands it to me and then holds the curtain shut as much as possible, keeping her eyes pinned to the floor like she's trying to give me privacy.

I pull my arms through the stretchy sleeves, careful not to snag the soft material.

Mom looks up at me. "The color is beautiful on you."

I glance down at myself. I'm wearing a tent. "It looks like one of your maternity dresses. No offense."

“So that’s a no,” she says. She hands me a pair of pants—black jeans—and a gray long-sleeved shirt.

I don’t take the dress off. I sit down on the edge of the chair and slide each of the pant legs over my feet. I can’t bend over enough to step into them. I inch them halfway up my thighs, stand up, and hoist them over the brace. Even if I pull them up as much as I can, they won’t button over the middle of me. I lift the dress enough to show her.

Mom sighs and shakes her head, as if I’m happy about the fact that so far nothing fits.

I take off the dress and pull the shirt over my head. It gets caught on the top strap, so Mom has to help me.

I stand up and look at myself in the mirror. The long-sleeved shirt is thin and tight, like a layer of tracing paper showing off an outline of my brace. My plastic hips jut out through the pants that won’t button, and the ventilation holes scattered across my stomach make me look like a block of Swiss cheese covered in cloth. The part of the brace that goes into my armpit pushes against my boob so it looks dented. I turn around. It’s even worse in the back. Under the fabric, the straps look like three bulging humps. The bottom of the brace is long and flat, so I have a cardboard-box butt. “Pants are out,” I say.

“You can’t wear a dress in February. We live in Massachusetts!” she says. “We need to find you a few pairs of pants.”

“Good luck with that.” I mean, I get that pants are practical, and in general, for life, I’m pro-pants. But pants plus a back brace: No. Fail. Abort mission, unless you don't mind looking like you have a pancake butt.

Mom hands me a black dress. I slide it over my head. From the front, it doesn't look that bad.

"It looks great. Really. It does." Mom nods her head quickly, trying to convince me she's right. I want to believe her, but when I look behind me, I can see an outline of the straps and hinges. I look like hammers and screwdrivers and other things that belong in a toolbox are poking out of me.

There are voices outside the fitting room, a mother and daughter, I think. Their words keep getting louder, like they're closing in on us. "Let me know if I can help you with anything else," a salesgirl says. All of a sudden, it feels a lot less private back here.

Mom pulls the curtain open. "Go look in the big mirror."

I shut it. I'm not walking out dressed like this.

"How are you doing in there, Rachel?" Justine asks. I can tell she's standing close, on the other side of the fabric.

"Okay," I say. My voice sounds squeaky and small, like it doesn't belong to me.

Mom opens the curtain, and I back into the corner. The brace makes a loud noise when it hits the plaster wall, like a car door slamming shut.

"Come out so you can see yourself in the big mirror," Justine says to me.

I don't move. I don't want her to see me from the back or the side.

"Go ahead, Rachel," Mom says.

I poke my head out first to make sure no one else is there, then walk down the hall to the three-panel full-length mirror. My hips lead the way. It looks like I'm wearing a hard, thick life jacket under my clothes, only the buckles are in the back. I'm lumpy and wide and weirdly shaped. I turn back around as fast as I can.

"This is a winner." Justine nods. "It's very flattering."

"Definitely," Mom says.

I catch them exchanging a look that tells me they're on the same team. I want to be on a team with Mom.

"I think you should get this one," Mom says. "Don't you?"

"Sure," I say, because I know it's probably the best we're going to find. Nothing in the mall is going to make the brace invisible, although that would be pretty awesome.

"We have it in purple too," Justine offers.

"We'll get both," Mom says.

"Just black," I correct her, because I think the lumps will stand out even more in a purple dress.

"Okay," Mom says. "It's a start."

I nod. "Yeah."

The curtain to the other dressing room opens and a girl who looks my age walks out. "I think we need to go down a size in these," her mother says, following her out of the fitting room. She's holding a pair of corduroys. "Don't you—" She stops talking as soon as she sees me standing there. "There's something wrong with that dress, honey," she says to me. She squints at my stomach like she's trying to figure out why I look weird. "It's all lumpy in the middle."

I don't say anything. I drop my head to my chin and walk as fast as I can into the dressing room.

Mom closes the curtain behind me and holds it shut while I pull off the dress. Then she takes off my brace, puts it in the pink bag, and covers it up with the sweatshirt. I change back into my regular clothes and sit down. The air is hot and thick and heavy against my chest, like I'm underwater and the waves won't give. I'm not wearing the brace anymore, but it's still there and it's not going away. Even if I never say it out loud or tell my friends or buy new clothes, the brace is real. It makes me look lumpy and wrong. I feel like no matter what I wear, I'll stick out. And I'm going to have to deal with it every day.

Mom sighs. "Why don't you go over to the Gap while I finish up here and pick out a few things that you think will fit? You can try clothes on at home and I'll return whatever doesn't work." She's whispering and rubbing my back in soft, soothing circles. "I'm sorry. I don't know why I didn't think of that before."

I nod. I know what she means by "before." "Mom," I say. "Thank you," and I mean it.

The sky is still blue when we get home. I carry my brace and shopping bags up to my room and drop everything in a pile by the door. It's all dresses and skirts. I can forget about looking like I'm not trying too hard ever again, because from now on, I'm always going to be dressed up like a fancy freak.

My jean shorts rub against the raw skin on my hips. The padding inside the brace pulls at me every time I take a step, stand up, or turn to the side. It's like walking around in a pair of bad shoes that rub and squeeze all day. I know it's just a preview, and I still need to be able to run in it for soccer.

That's when I remember the rubbing alcohol. As I head for the bathroom, I almost trip over the shopping bags piled up in front of my door. I turn around and kick them one by one across my room. It feels good to watch the perfectly folded clothes wrapped in tissue paper fly through the air and scatter across the carpet.

I open the bottle under the sink and soak a few cotton balls in the clear liquid until it's seeping onto my fingers. I sit down on the floor next to the tub. Mom is banging around in the kitchen, which means Dad will be home for dinner.

I lift up my tank top. There are blisters on my right and left hips. I hold my breath and place a wet cotton ball against my skin. It feels like the time Frannie burned my ear with a curling iron, but I press down harder.

I can hear Mom on the phone. She's sitting at the bottom of the staircase now, where everything echoes. "How do you think I'm doing? I don't understand, David. I felt so lucky. I felt thankful that they could fix what was wrong with me. I never complained about anything, and it was so much worse." Mom stops talking and listens to whatever Dad is saying. "Don't even say that. I can't think about it. Her brace is going to work. It has to. I'm barely making it through this." She listens again. "I think she should try, but I'm worried. It's going to be hard. And I hate to say it, but it could be . . . awkward." She pauses. "No, of course not. I mean, the orthotist said it was fine for her to play. I just don't think she realizes what it's really going to be like. But what can I do? Okay. We'll see you in a few minutes. I love you too."

So Mom thinks playing soccer in my brace is going to be awkward and that I'll be bad now. Great. That's perfect. Well, I don't care what she thinks. She's wrong. She doesn't know anything about soccer. She never even played. I'm going to find a way to be good, because I'm not giving it up. It's too important to me. Also, Hazel said we'd figure it out and she always tells me the truth, which means the truth is: I can do it.

When I get back to my room, I step around the scattered clothes and turn on the new playlist I started making last night. It's mostly pop with Motown mixed in. I always try to add mellow songs that sound dark and important, but I can't help that I like the peppy ones that make me smile and dance the most. It's just who I am music-wise.

My phone is buzzing and flashing. I have a group text from Frannie: The entire seventh grade is talking about you and Tate.

Serious? I write back.

No. I'm lying.

Swear on Chanel, I say, because it's the most important French thing that's coming to mind right now.

Haha, Hazel writes.

I swear, Frannie says. And shut up, Hazel.

Tate is totally going to ask you out. Everyone knows he likes you. Officially. Ladan told me.

I want to believe her, but I don't think I should get my hopes up until after Tate sees me in the brace.

☺☺☺, I write back.

The garage rumbles, opening and closing, and the door to the house slams shut. Dad is home, I write. GTG.

"Rachel," Mom yells. "Dinner." I need to get downstairs before she comes up here and sees my clothes all over the place.

The kitchen smells like tomato sauce or soup, something warm and comforting. Whatever Mom made is wrong for a hot summer night, but I don't mind.

Dad's been on call, so I haven't seen him since before I got the brace. I didn't realize how much I missed him until I see him standing over the counter, sorting through mail. He looks serious—black hair, black suit—and he keeps adjusting his glasses to read the fine print on whatever bill he's looking at. "Hello, Rachel," he says, looking up at me.

I run over and hug him.

He hugs back. "How was your day?" he asks.

I shrug.

"Rachel got a lot of beautiful new clothes for school, didn't you?" Mom answers for me. It's my cue to show them I'm grateful.

"Thank you for the clothes," I say, looking at Mom and then Dad. I walk over to the table and start setting three places.

"You're welcome," Dad says. Then he whispers something to Mom. They look at each other and smile. Dad rests his hand on Mom's stomach, so I know for sure that they're talking about the baby. I don't understand how Dad can be happy right now. Shouldn't he be worried about me? Shouldn't he be trying to make me feel better? I guess he assumes Mom is handling that.

"What did you end up getting?" Dad puts down the paper in his hand and looks ready to give me his full attention.

"Dresses," I say.

"Very nice," he says. "You like dresses."

"Yeah." I shrug. "I guess."

"Want to show me after dinner?" he asks. "I don't have to start my billing right away."

I shake my head. I know he's trying. But I don't want to put on a fashion show of my new outfits. "They don't look good. Nothing does. Today when we were in the fitting room, this woman told me that I look lumpy in the middle. And she saw the best outfit I tried on all day." I put the last fork in its place and sit down.

"Okaaay," Dad says. He looks at Mom for help.

"Don't look at me." Mom slams the metal cover on top of the pot.

"I suggest you give it some time," Dad says. "Adjustment to the brace can be difficult, but it does become manageable." He sounds like he's reading out of an orthopedic journal.

"I look like a freak. And there's no way I'm going to be good at soccer now, right?" I look at Mom. "But I have to wear the brace. So basically I can't really do the only thing I actually want to do. And I don't see how that will become manageable."

Mom and Dad don't say anything.

It's quiet and hot in the kitchen. We sit down at the table and eat in silence. I'm on my first bite of pasta when I realize I was counting on Dad to be on my side. I really need someone to get why I'm so sad, and it's not going to be Mom.

After dinner, Mom helps me back into the brace. I put on my soccer clothes, go outside with my ball, and start my regular warm-up.

Sprints. Every time I swing my arms back and forth, the

brace scrapes under my armpit. It hurts. But I don't stop. I run through the pain until I'm sweating and sticky.

I put the ball in front of me and try toe taps. The bottom of the brace digs into my legs each time I lift my foot and tap the top of the ball—*left, right, left, right.*

After I finish my warm-up, I practice juggling. I keep my feet low and try to stay in control of the ball, but my balance is off because of my brace, and it's hard to hop from one foot to the other without feeling like I'm going to fall over. I stop and try again. I kick the ball once off my laces and catch it. I go for two taps on the same foot, and then three. I switch feet and practice on the other side. Once I have that down, I go back to juggling from one foot to the other. I'm still wobbly, but I manage to hold on to the ball for a little longer.

Then I dribble across the yard, accelerate, and change direction, pulling the ball with me. Each time I speed up and turn, the brace rubs against my hips. I don't care that it hurts. I push through. I'm not giving up. I'm playing, and I'm going to be good, even in the brace.

six

THE NEXT DAY, after practice, Mom drives Hazel, Frannie, and me back to our house for a sleepover. The whole way home, I keep trying to think of ways to tell Frannie about the brace, because I'm doing it tonight. I have to wear it for eight hours today and ten tomorrow. There's no way I could hide it from her, even if I wanted to, which I don't. I'm ready to talk about it. Also, it's my first night sleeping with it on. True fact: I did not want to have a sleepover tonight, but Frannie insisted, and when I asked Mom to nix it, she said no, and that I shouldn't run away from my problems. But she also said I should lean on my friends for support, and I think she might be right about that part.

The plan for the rest of the day and night is to watch *Dirty Dancing*. We rotate the same dance classics at every sleepover—*Girls Just Want to Have Fun* and *Footloose*. They were

Frannie's mom's favorite movies, and they would play on repeat in the background of everything, even after she got sick. I'm not sure if that's the right word to use, but I don't know what else to call it. "Mental illness" is what Mom called it, but that sounds worse than sick. It sounds like a secret illness hidden away in her head.

Hazel and I are the only ones who know how Frannie's mom died—that she took too many pills because she was sad and trying to make herself feel better. It was an accident. Mom told me it wasn't a regular decision, the kind Frannie's mom would have made when she was healthy. But Frannie doesn't like to talk about things that are wrong in her life. Most of the time she pretends they're not there.

I personally like watching the same happy dance movies over and over. Sometimes it's nice to watch a story where I know all the answers, even if none of them are real. Plus, it makes Frannie happy, and we know every word, so we only sort of have to pay attention.

When we get home, Frannie takes off her soccer stuff and throws it into her gym bag. Frannie is all muscle and curves, and out of nowhere it seems like she's a B-cup too. I don't remember Frannie ever going into the bathroom to change. That's Hazel's move. She's in there now.

Hazel comes out of the bathroom in her pajamas. I used to think having boobs was bad, because Frannie was flat too and I was the one who was different. I've always been a little ahead of them. But now Frannie has them too and Hazel is the only one who doesn't. It's weird how one minute you can be like everyone else and the next you're the one who doesn't fit in.

"So, I know we have a few days off, but we should still practice. You need to get ready for your first game on offense!" Frannie sounds so excited.

I look at Hazel. Her shoulders fall, like her whole body is sighing in support of me. It makes me feel better, like I'm not alone in this.

"I have to tell you something," I say to Frannie.

"What's up?"

"I have to wear a back brace," I say. Her face doesn't change. "All day. Every day. Even during soccer. For the next six months or a year, maybe. It looks bad. And I don't know how I'm going to play in it like I do now. I mean, I'm allowed to. I tried last night, and I think I can. But I don't know. It's going to be hard."

"Why do you have to wear it?" she asks.

"I have scoliosis."

"I think my aunt had that. She didn't have a brace or whatever they did back then, but I'm pretty sure my mom told me about how she had to go to the doctor for it. At least, I think it was my mom who told me that." Frannie shakes her head. "I'm forgetting everything about her already." She clenches her jaw like she's trying not to cry.

I sit down next to Frannie. I try to figure out the right thing to say, but none of the words in my head sound good enough. Hazel doesn't say anything either. No one tries to fill the space by talking. We sit there in the quiet.

Frannie takes a deep breath. "It will probably help your posture, right?" she asks.

"Yeah." I nod.

"So if you think about it, it's not all bad."

"I guess not," I say. I hadn't even considered that there might be good things about having a back brace, but posture feels important. Maybe there are other advantages I just can't think of right now.

"Can I see your brace?" she asks.

"Sure," I say. "Will you help me with it?" I look at Hazel.

"Wait, when did you find out?" Frannie asks Hazel.

"A few days ago. It was a total accident. I swear."

"Oh. Okay." Frannie nods, like she's glad she wasn't left out for too long or on purpose. "On a scale of one to drama queen, how bad is it?" she asks Hazel.

"Seven-ish." Hazel doesn't look at me. "But Rachel still looks really pretty."

"Well, it doesn't cover her face," Frannie says. "Wait, does it?"

"No," I say, smiling.

"That would be bad." She smiles at me. "See, it could always be worse."

I know she's right.

I don't go to the bathroom to change, but I don't take everything off either. I keep myself covered up, slipping my special tank top over my head while sliding my soccer shirt down until I can step out of it. I put on a regular bra and then put the brace around me. I try to ignore the sound of the metal hinges rattling against the plastic.

Hazel struggles to get the first strap closed. "Are you okay?" she asks.

"Mm-hmm." I keep my eyes shut so she can't see that they're starting to water.

"Let me do that." Frannie pushes Hazel out of the way. "No offense, but I'm the muscles of this group." I can't help but laugh. "Watch and learn." She pulls the brace shut in what feels like three seconds. It's even tighter than when Mom did it. And even though it hurts at first, after a few minutes, it's much more comfortable because there isn't any extra space between the padding and my skin. It doesn't rub as much. I'm starting to get used to being enclosed inside of it.

"Okay. I definitely thought it was going to be way worse. It's only bad in some places." Frannie points to my hips.

I pick up my sweatshirt and cover myself as fast as I can. When I look down, all I can see is fabric. I like being hidden, even from myself.

"And don't worry. No one is going to think you have a weird

body or anything," Frannie says. "They'll think you're wearing a cast. It doesn't even look like it's part of you. It looks totally separate."

"How is that a good thing?" I ask.

"People get casts all the time, and it's no big deal. It's a normal thing that happens. If anyone at school asks, say you got hurt, and everyone will feel bad for you."

"I guess that's better than being made fun of."

"Definitely," Hazel says. "Much better. Plus, you're going to have a really popular BF, so that will definitely help your status."

"And you're still going to be good at soccer," Frannie says. "You have the best footwork on the field."

"Um, hardly," I say.

"Okay. Not yet. But you're going to."

I nod. "Okay."

"Have you tried kicking the ball with it yet?" Frannie asks.

"I worked out last night, but I only practiced kicking with my right leg. I can hardly move my left hip."

"Yeah. You're going to need to get really good with your right foot," she says. "Get dressed."

"Now?" Hazel asks.

Frannie nods. "Now." She looks at me. "You're still going to start."

I smile and open my dresser to find clean shorts and a T-shirt. Frannie thinks I can be good at soccer, even in my brace. I could have the fastest feet on the team. That could be my thing.

Frannie and Hazel spend almost an hour helping me practice chipping and pinging. My body is tense inside the brace and my right foot feels floppy and weak, like I'm not fully in control. When I want to give up, they root for me and push me to keep kicking until I feel confident, and like maybe I could still start and play forward. By the time we go back inside, I'm not as nervous about soccer. Plus, I have the best friends ever. So school might not be that bad.

Two days later, I'm stuck in the brace for fifteen hours. That's nine hundred minutes. I've got seven hundred and eighty-two down, one hundred and eighteen to go.

It's weird to wish time away, to count the seconds, waiting for the ones that belong to me. It feels especially wrong because it's the end of summer, and if everything were normal, I'd want time to slow down.

Up in my room, I stare at my laptop screen, willing someone, *anyone*, to sign on to chat and distract me for a few minutes, but it isn't working. It's hot and sticky inside the brace. I want to take it off and let my skin breathe for a little while, but Mom already told me I need to practice wearing the brace straight through, because after I finish adjusting, every minute I spend out of the brace gets deducted from my one free hour. And I can never take extra minutes or hours off, because we have to do everything possible to make sure I don't need surgery. I want to know what makes surgery so bad, so I search "What happens when you have surgery for scoliosis?"

I scroll through the results looking for answers. First I open "Spinal Fusion Success Stories," which has profiles of two smiling girls who both had surgery. One runs competitive cross-country now and the other still loves to horseback ride. They're both healthy and really strong. Also, they're friends with each other, which is cool. I go back to the results and open a different link about "the complications and potential risks associated with a spinal fusion." They're listed in bold: **Infection. Nerve damage. Blood clots.** Not good. There are no stories or pictures of happy teenagers here. Just big, scary words with short descriptions that make me want to stay in my brace, where it's safe, and not cut any corners, not even small ones.

I search again and look through the images this time: x-rays, before-and-after shots, and a diagram of a curved spine. I zoom in on a picture of surgical tools holding open something red. It's the inside of someone's spine! I shut my screen.

"Surprise! I'm here!" Hazel's voice makes me jump up off the bed a little. She's standing in the doorway.

"Hi!" I say. "Wait, what are you doing here?"

"My mom was coming over to drop off a bunch of baby stuff. You're not mad that I came over, are you?"

"Shut up," I say.

"Okay, good." She smiles like she's relieved. "We're leaving for Long Island in T minus two hours. I won't be back until Monday, and we start school on Tuesday. I can't believe it's so soon!" Her voice gets way high, like she's excited about seventh grade and soccer and Kyle and all the same things I'd be squealing about if I wasn't scared about starting school in the brace. "Um, we need to talk about first-day outfits. How have we waited this long?"

"I know!" I say. "I'm freaking out. My new clothes are all for fall."

"Same with me!" she says. "It's like, hello, why can't the weather know that school is starting and respond accordingly?" She claps her hands together, like she's trying to get excited. "Okay, show me the options."

"I don't even know what I got." I grab on to the bedpost and pull myself up in one motion. I'm better at maneuvering around without getting jabbed by the brace. As soon as I'm standing in front of the pile of bags and torn tissue paper, I realize there's a reason everything is still on the ground. I don't think I can reach down and pick the clothes up. I bend forward and try to ignore the brace digging into the top of my thighs, as well as the feeling that I'm about to topple over.

"Let me do it," Hazel says. She picks everything up off the ground. "What's going to happen when you go out of bounds in a game?" she asks. "You have to be able to pick the ball up really fast and throw it back in."

"I'll figure it out," I say. I've been so focused on running and kicking that I completely forgot bending down would be an issue too.

"I know you will." She holds up a purple skirt. "This is cute," she says.

It's one of the things I didn't try on, so in my head I can pretend it looks really good. I pick it up by the elastic waistband and put it next to a black tank top and a very thin gray sweater that looks like the kind of thing I might be able to hide under. "With this?" I ask.

She tilts her head and her eyebrows scrunch together. "Yeah. That's a winner."

"Not trying too hard?" I ask.

She shrugs, and I guess I know she's right. I can't have everything.

I change into the outfit, and as soon as I'm done, Hazel says, "I love it."

"Yeah? I don't look weird in the middle?" I ask, because after what happened with that mom in the fitting room, I'm nervous about how I look in clothes.

"No way," she says. "Two thumbs up."

I open my closet door and look in the mirror. She's right. I look good. The skirt is a little too short, since I put the elastic part above my fake hips, but no one can see that because of the sweater, which I grabbed on our way out of the store. It's amazing—long and a little tighter at the bottom, so the middle puffs out enough to almost cover up my hips and straps. And it's really thin, so I can probably pull it off without anyone saying, "Aren't you hot in that thing?"

We piece together a few more outfits before Hazel's mom knocks and says that they're leaving in five minutes. I look at the clock: the hundred and eighteen minutes are up. It turns out wearing the brace is a lot less painful when you aren't counting and you're with your best friend.

"Can you help me out of it?" I ask Hazel.

"Have you tried getting out by yourself?"

"I can't." I take off my sweatshirt, reach around, and grab for the strap. "See?"

"Try pulling from the middle of the strap, instead of reaching for the end."

I dig my nails into the Velcro and pull from the middle like Hazel said. I tug at it until the whole strap comes undone. It works. I can't believe it. I do the same thing with the other two straps and take off the brace without any help.

I drop it on the ground and hug her. "Thank you," I say. "I would have never thought of that on my own."

"No big deal," she says.

Only it is.

The next day, I have to wear the brace for twenty-three hours. Twenty-three hours is a long time to do anything, especially when it's something you hate. But I don't have a choice. I have to suck it up and try not to think about it. So as soon as I wake up I put together a back-to-school playlist, because that always makes me happy. I pick songs from '80s movie soundtracks that are uplifting but not too distracting. And I'm pumped when I finally get to listen to it, because I think it's going to be really good for doing homework.

Then I go outside with the soccer ball. I know I shouldn't work out too hard the weekend before my first practice in the brace, but I have to be able to pick the ball up as fast as I could before. The game clock doesn't stop when the ball goes out of bounds. Those few seconds could mean everything. Also, I know I can do this. I have super long arms, and we're using size five regulation soccer balls this year, which means they're bigger and I don't have to bend down as far to get the ball. Two thumbs up for that.

I drop the ball on the ground in front of me and take a deep breath. I bend my knees and reach down, but the brace digs into my upper thigh. I stand up and try again. This time I keep my knees straight, bend forward, and grab the ball. It pinches a little in that same spot. I do it over and over until I have it down.

After I'm finished practicing, I go into the kitchen to get a glass of water and accidentally slam into the counter. My brace makes a loud cracking noise when it knocks against the granite, but the impact doesn't hurt me like it should. I don't feel anything. As soon as I realize that, I can't stop smiling, because out of nowhere I found another good thing about wearing a back brace. I can run into things without getting hurt. It's like armor. When I think about the brace like that, it almost feels like a secret weapon.

seven

THE NIGHT BEFORE the first day of school, Mom is standing at the kitchen counter reading one of her DIY home-decorating magazines. "Rachel," she says, stopping me on my way upstairs. "How are you feeling about tomorrow?"

I shrug. "Fine, I guess. Hazel helped me pick out an outfit."

"That's great."

"Yeah, it is," I say, because I know I'm lucky to have good friends.

"You're going to talk to Coach Howard before practice, right?"

"Why? There's nothing to talk about. I'm playing even better now. Okay, not everything is better. But my footwork is."

"Rachel—"

"It *is*," I say.

"I believe you, honey, and I'm proud of how hard you've

been working to get ready for soccer. But you have to tell Coach Howard about your *you know what*," she says, pointing to my brace. "You're still adjusting. You will be for another—" She looks over at Jules's chart, which is tacked up on her half bulletin/half chalkboard.

"Today is the last day of 'physical adjustment,'" I say, before she can find the answer. "So, you can take that down now. Thanks."

"No one knows what it is."

"It says 'Rachel Brooks's Brace Schedule' at the top, so actually everyone knows exactly what it is. Can you take it down? I mean, I'm done adjusting, so I don't think we need to advertise it in the kitchen anymore."

"Advertise," she says. "That's a little dramatic." She walks over to the bulletin board, unpins the paper, and puts it in the recycling bin. "Better?"

I nod. "Thank you."

"You need to talk to your coach about the brace tomorrow before practice," she says. "She needs to know it's important."

"Fine," I say.

"Also, you're going to have to miss practice on Wednesday. You need to have x-rays taken."

"I can't miss soccer this week. We have a game on Friday," I say. "Can you please change the appointment?"

She shakes her head.

"Mom. Please."

"We need to make sure the brace fits. It's a priority. And this was the only appointment they had this week. So you need to tell your coach you won't be there," she says. "Are you listening, Rachel?"

"Yes," I say. "I'll tell her the brace is your only priority." I walk upstairs before she has a chance to say anything else that I don't want to hear.

I plop down on my bed and text Frannie: Telling coach tomorrow ☹

Want me to go with you? she writes back.

OMG! Yes. Please. I hadn't even thought to ask her. Can you go at lunch?

Totes!!! she says. Done and done.

eight

WHEN MY ALARM goes off in the morning, I want to stay in bed and pretend it's not the first day of school. I couldn't sleep last night, which is weird because so far I haven't minded sleeping in my brace. I kept rolling around trying to find a comfortable position and trying not to think about how nervous I was for today.

I climb out from under the covers and peel off the brace. My muscles are so stiff, I wouldn't be surprised if I heard myself creak and then crack in half. I lean against the edge of the bathtub and turn on the water, waiting for steam to fog up the mirrors. My back is throbbing. I need this shower so I can move and breathe and feel like me again.

I reach behind the glass door. The water is freezing. I wait a few seconds and then try again. Still cold. "Mom . . ." I shout as loud as I can.

"I know," she yells back. "Ed is on his way over to fix it. I'm sorry."

I look in the mirror. Disaster. My hair is tied back in a tight bun, but wispy pieces hang around my swollen eyes from tossing and turning. It's not a good look. I can't go to school like this. I hang two towels over the shower door and step in, letting the icy water pour over me until I've finished washing my hair and the goose bumps on every inch of me start to ache. I shut off the faucet, shivering from the water dripping down my arms and legs, and drape myself in towels. After I dry off, I stretch out my upper body using the foam roller Dad brought home for me. It helps a lot.

Once Mom is done helping me into the brace, I dot my eyelids with light pink shadow and braid my hair into a fishtail. I put on my new outfit and smile at myself in the mirror. I think I look pretty.

The first thing I see when I get downstairs to the kitchen is a giant bouquet of roses. I know they're not for me, because red roses are Mom's favorite. I like pink.

Mom is holding the phone between her ear and shoulder, laughing into the receiver as she arranges her breakfast. When she sees me standing there, she says, "I have to go, Sue." She listens to one last thing. "Okay, sounds good," she says and hangs up. "Can I make you something? Anything you want," she says to me.

I shake my head. I'm not hungry, and I don't like eating with the brace on, because the padding pushes against my stomach, and when I'm even a little full, it's hard to breathe.

"Take something with you in case you get hungry before lunch," she says. "You need to eat if you're going to play soccer."

I grab a few granola bars and a banana, because I know she's right about that.

When the phone rings again, Mom picks it up. "Hi, Ma," she says, smiling and sneaking off to the bathroom, her secret hideout.

Mom runs the water and I walk a little closer to the door so I can hear her. "It's a boy!" she says. That explains the flowers. "We're so excited. We're going to wait a few days before we tell Rachel. I don't want to burden her with one more thing right now. She already has so much going on." She really doesn't think I can hear her over the running water. I listen, waiting for her to say something else, but she's quiet. Gram must be talking. "I'm not telling her on her first day of school. I can't do that. We won't wait too long—just until she's back to being herself."

I wonder if Gram knows what I know: If Mom and Dad are waiting for me to go back to normal, they'll be waiting forever.

When I get to school, I see Frannie standing on the other side of the crowded courtyard with the forwards. I don't want to go over to them, but I don't see Hazel anywhere, and I can't stand here by myself. I don't see Tate either. Not that I'd go up to him, but I like knowing where he is.

"Rachel, over here!" Frannie waves to me. Her voice is loud enough that people turn around and stare.

I hold on to the green, leopard-print straps of my mostly empty backpack and keep my eyes on the ground. It still feels like summer, and I guess technically it still is. I've only taken a few steps and I'm already sweating under the thick layers of cotton and plastic. It's seriously hot inside the brace.

Frannie backs up, making space in the circle for me.

"Great color," Ladan says. "I love that purple skirt."

"Thanks." I smile at her, because even though I wish she hadn't drawn everyone's attention to me, I know she's being nice. I try to slouch a little, since I'm afraid they can see right through my shirt to the brace. I'm jealous of the way Ladan's turquoise V-neck falls and how her white jeans hug her legs like they were made for her. I wish I looked like that, like getting dressed was easy. Hazel slides into the circle on the other side of me.

"We're doing the long run today at practice," Ladan says.

"Who told you that?" Frannie glances at me to see if that's going to be okay.

I shrug, because I'm not sure. I've been running half a mile in my brace every other day as part of my training. But the long run is a mile.

"Josie," Ladan says.

"Obviously." Frannie rolls her eyes. "What's her deal? She's always hanging around Coach Howard."

"She's desperate. Also, can I just say what we're all thinking? I'm sorry that she has neck hair, but I don't want to look at it." Everyone laughs. Ladan is talking to Frannie, but she's looking at me. They all are. They look at me and then at each other, like they're passing messages with their eyes. *Something is definitely wrong with her. She's so not normal-looking right now. Did she swallow a cardboard box? How is she going to play soccer like that? I hope she doesn't think she's practicing with the forwards anymore. Who cares? It's Rachel Brooks. I always knew she was weird.*

I can't make it stop. I can't even prove it's happening. But I know I'm not imagining it, because Frannie and Hazel both look worried. They must know there's nothing they can say or do to make it better, because they don't do anything. Neither do I. We all just stand there and let them judge me.

The bell rings. No one rushes over to the building, because no one wants to seem like they're ready for school to start. Frannie and Hazel stand on either side of me like bodyguards, even after we have no choice but to start walking.

"I really don't feel like being all focused," Hazel says. "I mean, how can teachers expect us to concentrate?"

"At least you don't have math first," Frannie says.

"Excuse me," I say. "Double science."

"That's so not okay," Hazel says. Then she leans in and whispers, "Watch your skirt."

I reach for the hem in back, but all I feel is my leg. My skirt is hiked way up. My underwear is almost showing. I yank it down and turn around to see who's walking behind me. I don't recognize the girls, holding shiny, new folders and staring at me. They must be sixth graders. Still, they have this look in their eyes and smirks on their faces.

"Don't worry. No one else saw," Hazel says softly. "You caught it in time."

"Thanks for telling me." I swallow my words.

She smiles at me, and I try my best to smile back, because I really am grateful for Hazel.

Hazel waves bye to Frannie and me and walks into her class.

"Do you want to meet me outside Coach's office at lunch?" I ask Frannie.

"Yes, that's perfect," she says. "Don't worry. It's going to be great."

"I hope so," I say. "I'm really glad you're coming with me."

"Me too," she says.

The science lab is empty. There are folded pieces of paper at every seat with first and last names written in all caps. I turn around to make sure no one is looking before I adjust my skirt, pulling it down below my fake hips. I walk around the tables looking for my name. Every time I take a step forward, my skirt inches up. I push down on the elastic waistband again, but it won't stay put. I hate that I can't even feel it happening.

I stop as soon as I see "RACHEL BROOKS" next to "TATE" "BOWEN." My throat closes up. He wasn't on the class list. I read the names over and over and I wouldn't have missed his. Mr. Hsu must have made a mistake. I can't sit next to Tate in my brace for an hour and forty-five minutes.

I'm about to go to the nurse's office and fake a headache when Mr. Hsu walks into the room, followed by Tate. My heart sinks. I think about bolting out the door or re-applying my strawberry lip gloss or smiling really big, because one time Mom told me I look prettiest that way. I need to do something to distract him from my brace, but before I have a chance, he looks right at my stomach. His eyes stop and then jut away from me, across the room, like they're fleeing the scene.

I look down. It's not good. I'm clunky. I adjust my shirt. It doesn't make a difference. No matter what I do, something about me always looks off.

I sit down at our table and play with my hair. I don't look up when I see his bright green sneakers coming toward me.

Tate sits down next to me. "Hey," he says.

"Hey," I say, finally turning to look at him.

He's looking at Mr. Hsu. He doesn't glance over at me or call me "bus buddy." I hope that's just because Mom is driving me to school this year. He copies the information from the board into his notebook as fast as he can. Maybe this is how

Tate always acts in class. We've never been in the same one before.

I open my notebook and start copying everything down. I don't bother to read the words as I write them. I'm too busy trying not to think about the way he looked at me, the same way the forwards did and the woman in the dressing room. I try not to cry, but everything looks blurry and wet and I feel a few tears escape down my cheek. I catch them with my fingers and wipe them away as fast as I can, so it's like they never happened. A few drop onto my new notebook, seeping in and smudging the ink.

When Mr. Hsu drops a syllabus on my desk, I pick my head up and look at him. "We're going to jump in and start class off with an experiment." He paces around the room with his hands stuffed into his khakis, the way I've seen him walk around the boys' soccer field after school. He talks about the lab like it's a game we need to win. "You're sitting next to your lab partner. You're teammates now." He claps. "Get over to the lab tables and get to work."

It takes me a minute to piece Mr. Hsu's words together. Tate is my lab partner.

"How about I get the test tubes and eyedroppers, and you grab the rest of the materials?" I ask Tate.

He looks down at the list and then up at me. "That works."

I walk to the sink, rinse out the test tubes and eyedroppers, and bring them over to the table, where Tate is setting everything else up. He puts the instructions out in front of us, and safety goggles over his eyes. I put mine on my forehead like a headband, since it's not time to wear them, and then dry off everything I just washed with a paper towel. I add labels to each test tube and line them up. "Are you ready?" I ask.

Tate leans toward me, close enough so I can smell his shampoo. I bet it's called "Sporty Ocean Breeze" or something else that says "I'm a boy," because that's how it smells, in a good way. He pulls my goggles over my eyes. My stomach flips. "Don't be too cool for safety." He smiles at me. It feels like a sign, like maybe what I thought happened before didn't really happen.

"Thanks," I say.

Tate adds ten drops of grape juice into each test tube. Then I add ten drops of lemon juice.

"Have you talked to Adam since he left for college?" I ask.

"Yeah." He smiles. "Only once, but he's coming home if we make the play-offs—when we make it. Our team is unstoppable this year."

"That's huge," I say. "We're pretty good too. Maybe we'll both make the play-offs."

"You're still playing?" he asks.

"I'm starting, remember?"

"I thought I heard someone say you might quit or something."

What? "No. I'd never quit." I shake my head. It feels like my face is on fire. "I love soccer and being on the team."

He smiles at me. "I didn't really think it was true. That's not your style. They probably got confused."

I smile back. I should ask him who said it. But I don't think I really want to know.

"I seriously can't wait for Adam to get home. My parents don't get anything."

I nod. I think carefully about what to say, because I can tell he's sad about his brother being gone. "My parents don't get anything either. This morning I found out that the baby is a boy. But I only know because I heard my mom talking about it on the phone."

"I hate that," Tate says, like he's mad at Mom for me.

"Me too," I say. "I mean, hello, I can handle things."

"They'll probably tell you soon," he says.

"I hope so." I pick up a clean eyedropper, fill it with the liquid antacid, and add *one, two, three* drops to the first test tube. I stop as soon as the liquid changes color. "That one worked pretty fast," I say. "I mean, I think it did."

He shrugs. "I guess we'll see." His floppy brown hair falls in front of his eyes. He moves closer, so now our shoulders are barely an inch apart. My stomach gargles loud enough that he looks up. "Need one of these?" he asks, pointing from the antacids to me with his free hand.

I jump back before he can touch me.

"What was that?" he asks.

“Nothing,” I say, because even though it makes me seem really weird, I’m pretty sure it’s better than saying, “I don’t want you to touch my back brace.”

He fills up a new eyedropper with the next liquid antacid. I want to say something to cover the awkwardness, but I can’t think of anything, so it stays there, floating between us like a fart, smelling up the whole room, until science is over.

I’m planning on wearing my brace during gym, but when Mrs. Demetrius announces that we’re starting the year with a yoga unit, I realize there’s no way. Luckily Hazel is in my class. I don’t have to say anything to her. She looks at me and knows. I ask to go to the bathroom, and even though I don’t need Hazel’s help getting out of the brace anymore, she meets me there. It’s nice not to be alone.

It turns out that I really like yoga and it doesn’t matter that I’m not flexible. I can still do all the poses. I like Reverse Warrior the best, because when I lunge forward and reach up to the ceiling, all the muscles in my back and sides open up. It’s like a big yawn for my torso. But the problem with being out of my brace for the forty-five minutes of gym is that I’ve already used up all of my free hour for the day, since I took off the brace this morning to shower and stretch. And now I’m worried, because I need to shower after practice too.

I spend the rest of the morning waiting for lunch. The

whole time I'm in class, I keep thinking about how much I want to tell Coach Howard about my brace and get it over with already, but when the bell rings, I'm scared.

I meet Frannie by Coach's office like we planned.

"This is a fun surprise," Coach says, waving us in. Her office walls are covered with pictures and framed newspaper articles with action shots of her playing soccer.

I smile and take a deep breath. "I wanted to talk to you about something," I say softly.

She looks at me and nods. Then she looks at Frannie.

"I'm here for . . . I'm the friend," Frannie says.

Coach Howard smiles.

"I want to play soccer so badly," I say. "The thing is, I got a back brace for scoliosis, and I have to wear it all the time, even during soccer. But I'm still good. I swear. I've been practicing with Frannie."

"She really is," Frannie says, backing me up.

"I'm sorry I didn't tell you right away. I should have," I continue. "I mean, the person who made the brace said playing soccer would be fine, but I wasn't sure it was actually going to be. I needed to see for myself. Also, I didn't want to tell you because I don't want to lose my spot on the team. I love playing forward."

"Rachel—" Coach Howard says. *Please. Please. Please.* I cross my fingers. My heart is beating so fast it hurts. "You will always be welcome on this team."

"I knew it!" Frannie blurts.

"Thank you!" I say. "And I can still play forward?"

"Let's have you try it out at practice today. And we can see how it goes."

"Okay, that sounds good," I say, because even though I wanted her to say yes, she didn't say no. And if I play well at practice, I can stay a forward.

"I'm glad," she says. "Is running in the brace an issue at all?"

"No way. I've been running a lot. It's totally fine."

"Good. That's great." She sounds surprised. "Rachel, it's going to be your responsibility to tell me if that changes at any point. I need you to let me if you're in pain, or if I ask you to do anything on the field that's too much for you."

"I promise I'll tell you," I say. "I actually need to tell you one more thing right now. . . . I have to miss practice tomorrow. I need to get x-rays in my brace. And I know the rule: You don't practice, you don't play. But maybe you could make an exception, just this once, because I didn't find out about the appointment until last night and I tried to get my mom to switch it, but she said no."

Coach Howard nods. "You'll play on Friday. But from now on, I need you to let me know about your appointments in advance."

"Thank you! Thank you! Thank you!" I take a deep breath and let out all the air and the worry I've been holding inside. At least until practice.

After the bell rings, I head straight to the locker room. It smells like sneakers and fruity body sprays, and it's crowded with everyone getting ready for practice. I sneak to the back by the bathrooms and knock on the handicapped stall. Hazel unlocks it and opens the door for me, like we planned. Frannie is by the lockers in case anyone gets suspicious and starts asking questions. We all agreed that even though Frannie is better at helping me put on the brace, she's also better at thinking on her feet.

I need to take the brace off for a few minutes to stretch out between school and soccer. I pull open the Velcro straps one at a time. They sound like tires screeching across wet pavement. I put it on the ledge behind the toilet and start to stretch my back. It feels so good to be free even for a few minutes. I lift my undershirt, which has been riding up and making creases in my skin all day.

"Rachel!" Hazel covers her mouth. "Is it supposed to do that?"

I look down at the raw, blistered skin around my hips. "Pretty much."

"Did you tell your mom?"

"Yeah," I say. "She knows."

"Okay, good." Hazel takes a deep breath, as if the fact that my mom knows makes everything better. "This doesn't look safe," she says, picking the brace up from behind the toilet. "Wow. This thing stinks." She holds it away from her and coughs. "I can smell it from here."

"I don't know what to do," I say. "I can't clean it until I get home."

She takes a mini bottle of body splash out of her bag and sprays it on my brace. All I smell now is vanilla. "Better," I say.

"Definitely." She nods.

Once Hazel buckles me back into the brace, we change into our practice gear. She's done in a few seconds. It takes me longer, because the brace feels tight against my skin, like I'm being squeezed for juice. It's like that first time in the hospital every time. My muscles are in shock. Only now I know the pain will be gone soon, and in a few minutes, I'll start to forget the brace is there.

"Come on," Hazel whispers. "Let's get out of here."

"Sorry," I say. "I'm almost done."

"I don't want to miss everything. And I'm getting claustrophobic back here."

I'm not sure Hazel means it the way it sounds, like I'm holding her back. I hope that part is only in my head.

Finally I'm dressed, and we walk over to the lockers. Hazel sits down on the bench, and I stand next to her. I'd rather not sit unless I have to. Frannie smiles at both of us, and then Hazel smiles at me. We're in on something together, and even though it's my problem, it's not just mine.

"Anyone hanging out downtown on Friday after the game?" Ladan asks. She wraps her thick hair into a big bun on the top of her head, like a crown.

"Frannie, Rachel, and I are," Hazel says quickly.

"We are?" I don't mean to say it out loud, but the words slip.

"Um, yeah," she says. "Don't be stupid. We talked about it last night."

We definitely didn't, because I would have remembered that conversation, but I say, "Duh, of course. Brain fart." I look over at Frannie, but she must have gone to the bathroom, because she's not there anymore.

Ladan is talking about how we'll meet at Biscotti's. I try to listen, but I'm too busy thinking about how I have gym first period on Friday, which means I have to wear the brace downtown, because I'll have already used up my one free hour for the day.

On the way out of the locker room, I whisper to Hazel, "What was that all about?"

"Sorry," she says. "Kyle invited me last night. I meant to tell you this morning, but I forgot. There's been a lot going on today. But you'll come, right? I mean, you have to come!"

"Yeah, of course." I can't say no. Not when Hazel's been helping me so much. I know what she means by "a lot going on today"—we've both been too busy with the brace to talk about her boy situation.

"I was afraid we wouldn't be included if I didn't say yes right away."

I nod. "Can we please talk about Kyle?" I whisper. "This is really, really big news. It's practically a billboard."

"You think?" She's trying not to smile, but she can't help it. "I hope you're right."

"Promise you'll tell me if anything else happens?" I ask.

"I didn't think you'd want to hear about it today." She looks down at my brace.

"I want to," I say. "Really." I don't want the brace to get in the way of the things that truly matter to me.

She smiles.

I walk onto the field with Hazel and Frannie. I'm wearing a shirt that's a little loose at the bottom so the edges of the brace don't stick out.

"Rachel." Coach Howard waves me over as soon as she sees me.

A few of the girls whisper to each other, and I'm pretty sure I hear one of them say my name. I wish I knew which one of my teammates told Tate I was quitting. I try to block that out. Nothing on the field has changed. I still have a chance to play forward. I can still be good. Even Frannie thinks so, and she wouldn't lie about soccer. I walk straight over to Coach.

"I spoke to your mom this afternoon," Coach Howard says.

"She called you?" I ask.

"Yes. She wanted me to know that you're still adjusting to your brace."

"That's not true." I know it doesn't matter what I say right now because Mom is my mom and an adult, and Coach Howard is obviously going to believe her over me, but I can't stop myself. I can't believe she did this to me. "I've been practicing every day."

"Your mom told me that too," she says. "I still want you to take it easy, okay?"

"I don't need to. And I'm done adjusting."

"You're such a strong player, Rachel. I see how dedicated you are. I want to make sure you're taking care of yourself."

"I am. I swear. I'm stretching a lot. And I'm still really good. My footwork is even better than before."

"I bet," she says. "We're doing the long loop today. I wanted to give you the option to sit it out. And then after, I'm going to have you practice with the defense."

NO! That's not fair. She isn't even giving me a chance to prove I can do it. "I thought I was going to at least get to try. You saw how well I played on offense the last few practices." I keep my voice soft and steady, even though it's the opposite of how I feel.

"I did. I was impressed," she says. "But I've given this a lot of thought since my chat with your mom, and I'd like you to go back to playing defense for right now. We can reconsider having you play offense after our game on Friday."

I bite down on my lip and swallow hard. "I don't need to sit out of the run. I'm good to go." I'm afraid if I say anything else right now, I'll cry, and I can't, so I walk away.

We're about halfway through the long run and pretty far into the woods when I start to fall behind the rest of the team. The brace isn't even rubbing against me. It's fine, and I can keep up with everyone else. It's just that I don't really want to. I did everything Mom asked. I took responsibility for the brace and talked to Coach Howard. I don't understand why she had to call anyway.

Frannie runs backward, retracing her steps, to find me. "You okay?" she asks, trying to catch her breath.

"No," I say, and as soon as I do, I'm crying.

"Does the brace hurt?" she asks. "Do you need me to take it off?"

I shake my head. "I'm playing defense. I got demoted."

"What? Why?" Frannie sounds mad.

"Because my mom called Coach, even though I said I'd talk to her."

"Not okay. No. Just no!" she shouts. "That's not fair." It feels good to hear her say that it's not what I deserve. I take a deep breath and wipe away my tears. "I can't believe Coach is not even giving you a chance," she says.

"You haven't heard my mom talk about the brace," I say. "She acts like it's the only thing that matters. I mean, I know how important it is. I'm wearing it and I'm being careful. I just don't want it to get in the way of everything."

"Then don't let it," she says.

"Do you think we can still catch up with everyone else?"

"If you want to."

"I do," I say.

"Then let's go!" Frannie sets a fast pace, and it doesn't take us very long to rejoin the rest of the team. By the time Coach Howard can see us again, we're running with the pack, and it's like nothing even happened.

The good part about the long loop is that more than half of practice is over by the time we're done running and stretching. We only have time for a few rounds of two-on-one drills. I'm glad about that, because I feel like every person on the team is whispering about me while they're waiting for their turn.

Not that I blame them. Here's the story of my life at soccer today: I've been dropped from the offense, and I can't really kick the ball. I keep trying, but my left hip hardly moves, and my right leg is tired and mushy from the run.

Hazel and I go up against Josie in the two-on-one drill. I steal the ball from her pretty easily, dribble away, and pass to Hazel. Only it looks like I've never kicked a ball before, because it goes way up high and not in her direction.

After the play is over and Hazel and I walk to the back of the line, she stands next to me and doesn't say anything. Not even normal things about homework or dinner or Kyle. I have this feeling the whole time I'm on the field that everyone else is on the team and I'm not. I'm the thing they're all laughing at.

When Frannie's dad drops me off at home, Mom is in the kitchen packing up her knitting supplies. "How was your first day?" she asks, inspecting a ball of blue yarn.

"Fine." I open the fridge and take out a bowl of fruit.

"I want to hear about it when I get back. I'm running to knitting group. Dad will be home early—on the early side," she corrects herself. "There's dinner in the oven. You should eat together."

"Okay," I say. "Thanks." I wish Mom would look at me and see that today wasn't fine. I want to tell her that practice was horrible partly because of her, and everyone is going downtown on Friday and I want to go too, but not in my brace. But by the time I find the words, the garage door is opening and Mom is gone.

I put on my new homework playlist. I let the music sink in and pick me up.

When Dad gets home a few hours later, it all spills out. He listens to me talk and nods between bites of salmon and broccoli. When I finish, he wipes his hands and reaches into the secret inside pocket of his suit jacket, where he used to keep butterscotch candies for me when I was little. He takes out a prescription pad, writes something down, and hands it to me.

Rachel Brooks should be excused from gym on Friday. She cannot participate.

"Now you can at least go downtown without the brace," he says. "Does that help?"

"So much," I say.

"Good." He takes another bite of his dinner.

"Dad," I say.

"Yeah?" he asks.

"Thanks."

"Nothing to it."

I wish it were true. I wish all of my problems were the kind that Dad could fix.

nine

ON WEDNESDAY, MOM picks me up from school twenty minutes early so we can get to the hospital on time. When we get there, Mom takes out her knitting and I put in my headphones and listen to a soccer playlist from last year while we wait for someone to call my name. After an hour, I'm summoned to pose for the same two x-rays they always take—one from the back and one from the side. Only this time I'm wearing my brace when the x-rays are taken. I like the hospital a lot more now that I have a brace. I get to keep my bra, underwear, and tank top on underneath it, and I wear two gowns while we go through the halls and take the elevator downstairs to see Jules.

We don't have to wait that long before she walks into the room. "How's everything going?" she asks, looking right at me.

I shrug. "Okay, I guess."

"How's your skin? Any redness or blistering?"

"Yeah," I say. "Kind of a lot."

"Would you mind showing me?"

I take off my robes and unbuckle my straps. I pull the brace off and lift up my shirt so Jules can see the raw patches of skin on my hips.

"Hmm." She adjusts her glasses and leans forward, taking a closer look. "I suspect this is your skin adjusting, and that after these blisters heal, you shouldn't have a problem, but I want you to let me know if that's not the case, so we can make some changes if we need to. I want to make sure you're as comfortable as possible."

"That's great," Mom says.

"Are you in any other pain?" Jules looks right at me when she asks.

"It still hurts right after I put it on."

"That's okay. But if the pain persists for more than a few minutes, you should let me know." She looks at me and then at Mom. We both nod.

"How does the brace feel during soccer?"

I shrug. "The same as the rest of the time."

She nods and her eyebrows go up, like she actually gets how hard it is. "Is there anything else?"

"Um, yeah," I say. "It kind of smells."

Jules smiles and opens the big cabinet by the door. She grabs a handful of small packets. They're pads of rubbing alcohol. "Stick these in your backpack so you don't have to wait until you get home to wipe down your brace. That should solve the problem."

"Thanks," I say.

"So, I reviewed your x-rays and everything looks great," Jules says. "The brace is an excellent fit. I'd like to trim down the piece that goes under your arm as well as the bottom edge, if you don't mind waiting a few minutes. You can stay here. It won't take long. But I think it will make the brace slightly more comfortable for you."

"Um, yes, please." I smile and nod.

Jules takes my brace in the other room.

When she comes back, she buckles me into the brace. I can feel the difference right away. There's more space between the plastic edge and my armpit. My boob isn't dented in anymore. And when I try to sit down and bend over, the bottom edge doesn't pinch the top of my thigh as much. "Thank you," I say to Jules. I can already tell the little changes are going to make a big difference.

As soon as we get in the car, Mom says I can play my music, which is amazing, because she usually listens to the traffic report on the way home from Boston. We're in the middle of the first song—"Here Comes the Sun"—when Mom says, "So, Dad and I found out the baby's gender."

"Oh yeah?" I try my best to act like I have no idea what she's going to say next.

"You already know?" She glances over at me like she's checking to make sure she's right. "How?"

"I heard you tell Gram it's a boy."

She claps her hand over her mouth. "I'm so sorry, honey. Dad wanted me to tell you right away. I should have listened to him." She shakes her head. "I wasn't trying to keep it a secret from you. I just wanted to wait until we had a few minutes alone to talk about it in case you had any questions."

"I don't." I shake my head. "I'm excited about having a brother."

"Okay, good," she says. "Well, if you do want to talk about anything, we can, whenever you want. I'm really sorry. I feel terrible."

I nod, because I know she means it. I just wish Mom would feel this bad about the things that actually upset me.

ten

I SKIP GYM on Friday with Dad's note and spend the whole period in the library working on my science homework.

After school, I change into my uniform. I told Mom she shouldn't come to the game. I haven't gotten better since Tuesday. Not even a little. I missed practice on Wednesday. And on Thursday, I was basically the same—not so great. I didn't even tell Mom that I'm back to playing defense—if I'm lucky. I said it would be better if she picked us up after the game was over and then dropped us off downtown. Still, when I step onto the field in my cleats, I expect to see her next to Hazel's mom.

In the huddle, Coach Howard talks about teamwork and manning the goal and being aggressive. She reads off the starting forwards and midfielders, and I stare at the grass. She doesn't call my name.

“Now on to defense,” she says. I hold my breath. I know it’s a long shot, but I still want to be picked. “Angela on the left, Josie in the middle, and let’s start with—” Coach Howard pauses before she reads the last name on her list of starters. “Hazel on the right.”

My stomach drops. It’s official. I’m on defense, and I’m not even starting. I squeeze Hazel’s hand and smile at her. I wish I could be happy for her in a real way, the way she was happy for me when I got picked to play forward, but I’m so sad and jealous of her right now that I’m having a hard time feeling anything else.

I cheer for Hazel and Frannie and all my other teammates as they run onto the field, and I take my place on the sidelines. I don’t sit, because I’m already stiff inside the brace and I don’t want to make it worse.

Twelve minutes into the first half, nothing is happening on defense. Coach Howard puts me in for Angela on the left.

I jog onto the field doing butt kicks, though I try not to actually kick my butt, because it’s covered in plastic and it hurts. I’m excited I get to play. I want to do well and help us win, but I’m nervous I’m going to screw up and ruin things for the whole team, which would be a lot worse than not playing at all.

Ladan passes the ball to Frannie and one of the midfielders on the other team intercepts it. She dribbles toward me. I run forward as fast as I can. I do my best to shuffle and stay with her.

She drags the ball with the inside of her foot, hops, and pushes the ball with the outside of her foot to get around me and make a break for the goal. But I don't let her. I take the ball from her. Then I pivot and pull the ball with me, turning my back to her. I dribble left, which I know she's not expecting, and look around for an open player—Katrina. I'm about to ping the ball to her.

Then suddenly the girl behind me shrieks. "You need to watch that thing," she shouts, loud enough for everyone to hear.

I turn around. *What did I do?* She's holding her arm like she's in pain, and I realize I must have knocked into her with the back of my brace without realizing it.

The ref blows the whistle and runs over to us. The girl makes another loud breathing noise to show how much it hurts, and now I know she's making it into a bigger deal than it actually is.

"Everything okay over here?" the ref asks.

"Yeah. It's fine. I mean, she crushed me with that metal thing she's wearing, but I guess I'll be fine."

"Do you need to sub out?" he asks her.

She shakes her head.

I don't look up or around. Everyone on the field and on the

sidelines is staring at us and whispering to each other, probably about me.

"All right, then. Let's try to keep our hands to ourselves." The ref puts the ball down in front of her and blows the whistle.

The girl taps the ball to one of her teammates, runs past me, and gets the ball back before I can stop her. She shoots and scores.

Coach Howard keeps me in until the end of the half. Then she doesn't put me back in for the rest of the game. I sit on the sidelines while the other team scores two more times before the second half is over.

Everyone is in a pretty bad mood, since we lose 3–1. No one says a word to each other in the locker room.

I pull Hazel into the back by the bathrooms. "You rocked today," I say as softly as I can. She got an assist to an assist, and even though that isn't a real thing, it should be one. She would have had an actual assist if Ladan had taken a shot on goal when she had the chance, but Ladan passed to Saaya instead.

"Thanks for saying that," she whispers. "Don't worry about what happened. It's just the first game. It doesn't matter."

I want to believe her.

After I take a shower at home, I put on my favorite dress and a cropped jean jacket. I hide my brace in my new gym bag in the back of Mom's car. We're going to have a sleepover at Frannie's afterward.

Hazel and Frannie are whispering about something on the ride downtown. I'm in the front and they're in the back, so I can't hear anything they're saying. I hope they aren't talking about what happened at the game. Other than Hazel, no one has said anything about it to me. I guess I'm worried everyone thinks I'm the reason we lost today. I try to think about something else, something good and happy.

I get to hang out with Tate tonight. I smile. And it's Friday. I don't have to wear the brace to school until Monday, and that feels far away. It's funny how Friday night can trick you into believing the weekend will last forever.

Mom pulls up in front of Biscotti's. "Frannie's dad will pick you girls up."

"Thanks, Mrs. Brooks." Hazel opens the door, and they both get out of the car as quickly as possible.

"Hold on a second," Mom says to me.

"What?" I ask, checking to make sure my friends haven't gone inside without me. They're standing by the door waiting.

"I'm going to drop your brace at Frannie's, but Rachel, you'll be out of it for extra time today." She's giving me this look I've only seen one other time that I can remember—when I didn't tell her about getting a "C" on a math test at the beginning of last year.

"I'm making up the time tomorrow," I say. "I already planned it out."

"This is a special occasion," Mom says. "Not a regular thing."

"It's ten minutes," I say.

"You have to get used to the routine of being in the brace."

"It's *ten minutes*." My words taste bitter the second time.

"It matters. Every second counts." Mom's voice sounds angry. "You want the brace to work, trust me."

"I know," I say.

"Do you know what will happen if you don't wear it?"

"Surgery."

"But do you understand what that actually means?"

"I would if Dr. Paul explained anything to me," I say.

"Don't be rude."

I'm being honest.

"There are risks. Real ones."

"I know," I say. "I looked it up."

"I feel this shooting pain in my back right now, just from sitting in the car for too long," Mom says. "The brace is your one chance at preventing surgery. Lots of kids your age would do anything for that chance."

"I haven't messed anything up," I say. I jump out of the car and slam the door shut before Mom has a chance to say anything else.

"What was that about?" Hazel asks me on our way inside.

"Who knows?" I shrug it off. I'm excited to hang out with Tate and the team tonight, and I'm not letting Mom ruin it.

The forwards are crowded around one of the small tables by the window, sipping fancy coffee drinks topped with swirls of whipped cream. Ladan has done a costume change into cutoffs and a shirt that says "dweeb," which is the opposite of true.

I go to the bathroom with Hazel so I can look in the mirror one last time before Tate gets here. I coat my lips with strawberry gloss. "What were you guys talking about in the backseat?" I ask, because I want to know if they were talking about me.

"Oh. Nothing," Hazel says, looking away from the mirror and up at the ceiling.

"Seriously. You're the worst liar. Just tell me."

"Fine." She sighs. "We were talking about Kyle. You know how Frannie is sometimes really loud about the whole thing, saying I'm obsessed with him or whatever? I finally told her to shut up about it in front of the other girls, because they don't need to know I like him."

"I get that." I nod.

"I know you do," she says. "I always thought Frannie knew and talked about it in front of them anyway to annoy me."

"Um, I thought that too," I say.

Hazel shakes her head. "She seriously had no clue. I'm glad I said something. She pinky swore she'd stop talking about it in front of other people."

"Wow," I say. "That's awesome."

"Yeah." Hazel smiles at me. "It really is."

On our way out of the bathroom, she grabs my arm. Her long, pink nails pinch me. "They're here," she whispers.

I look up, and Tate and Kyle are standing at our table. Hazel pulls me over to the counter with the milks and sugars. There's a partial wall separating us from them, but we can hear everything they're saying on the other side.

"You drink coffee?" It's Tate.

"Um, yeah, I really need caffeine," one of the girls says. I can't tell who it is without looking.

"Oh," he says.

It's quiet for a minute.

"Does anyone know what's up with Rachel? She looks—*uhh*—different," Kyle says. I know it's him because it's not Tate, and he's the only other boy there.

"Yeah, I know," Frannie says. "She got really pretty over the summer."

"I didn't know you were a lesbian," Kyle says.

One of the girls giggles.

"So what if I was?" Frannie says. "I wouldn't have to deal with idiot boys."

"Whatever," Kyle says. "She looks weird."

My heart stops.

"So weird," the giggler says. "It's like her clothes don't fit right or something."

"It freaks me out to look at her," Kyle says.

I hate that Tate is here, listening to them talk about me like this.

"Can we talk about what happened at the game?" It's another girl's voice. I'm not sure who it is. I don't want it be Ladan, but it might be. "She *crushed* that girl. She really shouldn't be allowed on the field like that. She's dangerous. And she's not even good anymore."

"I can't go back there," I say to Hazel as quietly as I can.

"You have to," she whispers. She takes my hand and squeezes it. I squeeze back and lean against the empty wall. I know she's right.

"She didn't do anything to that girl," Frannie says. "That was a total act and you know it."

"We just want to know what's wrong with her," the person who might be Ladan says. "You don't have to be awkward about it."

"She has to wear a brace for her back. It's like a cast.," Frannie says. "You can ask Rachel about it. It's not a big deal She's cool."

"I bet," Kyle says.

"What's your problem?" Frannie asks.

"Chill out, Fran," the giggler says. "We're all just saying

what we think. You don't have to go all crazy psycho face on us."

Frannie doesn't say anything. I grab Hazel's arm. We can't stand here and let that girl call Frannie crazy, even if she doesn't mean it the way it sounds.

I walk out from behind the wall. Everyone stops talking as soon as they see me. It's dead quiet. I look at Ladan and then at Kyle. I don't look at Tate. "I have to wear a back brace for scoliosis," I say. "If you want to ask me about it, ask me." I have no idea where the words come from, but as soon as they're out there, floating around in the air, I feel them slap me in the face.

Nobody says anything.

"I don't have any questions, but I have a comment," Kyle says.

"I'm not taking comments," I say.

"Fine," he says. "Have you considered joining a freak show?"

"No," I say. I try to sound confident and fine, even though he's insulting me to my face. But I can't stay here, so I walk over to the door. I'm pretty sure Frannie and Hazel are right behind me, but I don't turn around to look because I can feel my face turning red and my hands shaking. I walk down the street until I know I'm completely out of sight.

When I turn around, Frannie and Hazel are there, and I'm so happy to see them. "You're not crazy," I say to Frannie.

"I know." She sounds hesitant, like she doesn't really know.

"You're *not crazy*," I say again.

"You don't look weird," she says.

I don't say anything, because I do.

Frannie sighs and then opens her mouth like she's about to say something else, but she doesn't. And I'm glad, because I don't want her to lie to me, and nothing she says will change how I feel.

"Do you think I'm dangerous?" I ask.

"I think the ref made a really bad call," Frannie says.

Hazel nods in agreement. "He never should have given that girl the ball. It made it seem like it was your fault when it wasn't."

"Really?" I shrug. "I don't know."

"Well, I do," Frannie says. "Anyone who freaks out about getting bumped by your brace is a total flopper drama queen. That's just a fact. Also, your brace is the best thing ever for keeping other players away from the ball. I think you need to start boxing people out with it. All you have to do is stick your butt out and bend forward a little and let that plastic put a few extra inches between you and the other players. Most people are either going to back up or get bumped. They aren't going to fake getting hurt and cry about it."

"I guess even if they do, it can't be worse than today," I say.

"Today would be hard to beat," she says. "I'm sorry it was so bad."

"Thanks," I say.

Frannie looks at her phone. "Ladan texted me."

"What did she say?" I ask.

"'Everyone wants to know why Rachel stormed off. No one was trying to make her cry. We were trying to be honest.'" Frannie looks at me like she's sorry she has to be the one to tell me.

"I got the same text," Hazel says.

Everyone is in there talking about me. I feel tears behind my eyes.

"Let's get out of here," Frannie says. "I'll call my dad to come get us now."

I nod.

"Wait. We're leaving?" Hazel looks down at her phone. "Kyle texted me too. He says he didn't mean it like that. He wanted to know what was up. And you look different than you did before. You know you do. But he's sorry."

"Okay," I say.

"You're good to go back in?" she asks.

"I can't," I say.

"Tate's in there," Hazel says. "He's waiting for you."

I shake my head. I feel stupid for not being over it. I know I'm making it worse, but I don't know how to make it better.

Frannie puts her phone to her ear, so I know she's calling her dad. We're going home early.

"I'm sorry," I say to Hazel.

"It's fine," she says, looking back down at her phone.

"Are you texting Ladan back?" I ask.

She shakes her head.

It doesn't feel fine.

eleven

IN THE MORNING, Frannie's house smells like cinnamon and butter. Her dad puts a stack of thick waffles and Vermont maple syrup on the table. "Perfect timing," he says as we stumble into the kitchen. "Come eat."

I take a bite of the waffle. It's perfect: crunchy on the outside and soft inside. I make sure to drink water between bites. I have to be careful I'm not getting too full inside the brace. I have a whole system now where I stop and wait to make sure I have space before eating more, and it actually works.

"Fran, we're leaving in ten," her dad says. "I'll drop you girls off at home on the way." He moves a bouquet of lilies from one counter to the other.

"K," Frannie says. She holds the syrup bottle upside down until her waffles are soaked in a sticky, sugary puddle.

Her dad looks like he could be going to play golf, but I can tell by the flowers and Frannie's tone that they're going to the cemetery to visit her mom. I look at Hazel, but she's looking at her phone.

"Does it get hot in there?" Frannie asks, pointing to my brace.

"Frannie—" Hazel stops texting and looks up.

"What did I do?" Frannie asks. "I want to know, and I keep forgetting to ask." She looks at me. "You don't have to talk about it if you don't want to, but I have questions and I'm not going to pretend I don't."

"I don't mind talking about it." I take another bite of waffle. I'm not full yet. I think I have room for two more bites, maybe three, before I officially have to stop. "It's sort of hot. I sometimes want to rip it off and jump in a cold shower. I probably will when I get home. But it's not always like that."

"Ugh. That sounds so bad," Frannie says.

"Yeah," Hazel says. She's not looking at her phone anymore.

"They—the people in the hospital—said I'd get used to wearing it all the time, but I don't know about that. I mean, maybe. My skin is a lot better now. My blisters are healing. I guess some things are easier now."

"Yeah," Frannie says. "You never know. You can get used to anything, if you have to."

Frannie is probably right about that.

~

I spend the rest of the day making brownies for the team bake sale on Monday, doing homework, and checking my phone to see if Hazel texts or calls. She doesn't. She's not on chat either. I can't decide if that's good or bad. I don't remember what she said she was doing for the rest of the day, and now I'm afraid she's hanging out with the soccer girls or doing something I can't because of my brace. If what happened at Biscotti's hadn't happened, I'd text Hazel and ask what she was up to, but I can't do that now without seeming desperate.

I shut off my phone and try not to think about it, which kind of works for an hour, but that's mostly because I'm outside trying to figure out the best way to dribble and stick my brace out at the same time. I'm planning to test Frannie's theory at our next practice. I figure out that in order to make it work, I have to bend my chest forward enough that the plastic part in the back of my brace sticks out, but not so far forward that I topple over or lose control of the ball. It's a balancing act, but I think I can do it.

As soon as I'm back inside, I give up trying not to think about what Hazel is doing and turn my phone back on. There are no little bells. No text messages or voice mails. Nothing.

A few hours later, I get a call from Hazel's house phone. "My phone was totally confiscated," she says as soon as I pick up.

"My mom at least had the decency to let me call you and Fran to tell you about it."

"Seriously?" Hazel's mom has never taken her phone away before, which is why I didn't even think of that as an option when I was worried earlier. "What did you do?"

"Um, nothing. I mean, she kept telling me to put it away, but Kyle was texting me, and I wanted to see what he was saying, which was not a smart move because she took my phone away right as I got a message from him. I never even got to see what he said. She said I could have it back when I could learn to manage it better."

"When is that going to be?" I ask.

"Apparently tomorrow after school," she says. "I can't even deal with her."

"Same," I say. "With my mom, I mean."

"I feel like you and your mom never fight about anything," she says.

I laugh a little. "Yeah, right," I say. "She got mad at me on Friday after you guys got out of the car because I was going to be out of my brace for an extra ten minutes."

"You've got to be kidding," Hazel says.

"I wish."

"Is it that serious?"

"I mean, I need to wear it as much as possible, but it's ten minutes, and it's not even about the ten minutes. She refuses to admit that this whole thing is actually hard for me. She acts like I should be *so* happy that I *only* have to wear a brace."

"That's really not okay," Hazel says. "She shouldn't be making it harder for you."

"Yeah, I'm pretty sure you're right," I say, because it sounds like the truth, and I think it might be. "Sorry about your phone."

"It's okay. It might be better. Guys like it when you play hard to get," she says. "Shoot. I'm getting the evil eye from the other room. I better go. I still have to call Frannie." After everything that happened at Biscotti's, I'm glad Hazel called me first.

"Moms are the worst," I say.

"Truth," she says. "See you on Monday."

twelve

WHEN I GET to school on Monday, I want to go straight to homeroom and hide, because I'm pretty sure that between the game and what happened at Biscotti's after, everyone is talking about how pathetic I am and how bad I am at soccer now. I can't do that, though. I'm here early to set up for the bake sale, and I'm not missing anything that has to do with soccer.

I walk across the cafeteria and over to the folding table. Frannie has dressed it up in black and red with a handmade sign that says *"Patisserie"* to make it authentic. The whole team is standing around the table dressed in soccer uniforms, including me. It's funny how wearing matching outfits really does make me feel like I belong.

Frannie is busy organizing baked goods and ordering people around. I put the tin of brownies I made on the table as Hazel walks over.

"Surviving sans phone?" I ask her.

"Barely." She smiles. "I tried giving my mom the silent treatment this morning, and halfway through breakfast, I forgot I was supposed to be ignoring her, because I needed her to sign a permission slip." We laugh.

Ladan walks over to us. "What happened to you guys on Friday? You just disappeared. We were all *so* worried."

Hazel looks at me like, *I told you so.* I get that "worried" is code for talking about us, and she doesn't want to be clumped in with me. I don't blame her for that.

"I got sick," I say. "It came out of nowhere. I'm so done with cafeteria hot dogs."

"Eww!" Ladan looks at Hazel and shakes her head. "So, anyway, we have to talk about you and Kyle and how you're basically almost BF/GF."

I want to take back what I said. I didn't even eat a hot dog. I just couldn't think of anything else to say. But it's too late to do anything other than stand here and feel like an idiot.

On our way to class, Hazel whispers, "I don't want to make you feel bad about what happened, but people would be over it by now if we had stayed."

"I know," I say.

"It's nothing. I mean, don't worry. It's really nothing."

If it were nothing, she wouldn't have to say it twice.

Frannie, Hazel, and I have the first bake sale shift. We're selling brownies and cookies and homemade macaroons from twelve until twelve fifteen.

Kyle walks over to our table. He looks right at me and says, "Hey, what's up?" like Friday never happened. Then he starts eating a brownie and talking to Hazel, like he doesn't realize he asked me a question. I hate that he doesn't care about the answer, and not just because he called me weird. I'm trying really hard to get over it for Hazel's sake.

"Hey, Rachel." It's strange to hear Tate say my name. It sounds like it belongs to someone else. Most of the time, I wish I had a cooler, more popular-sounding name, like Isabella or Madison. But in his voice, "Rachel" sounds important.

"Hey," I say.

"I was thinking we should, um, probably get each other's numbers, so we can text while we're studying for the science test next week," he says softly.

"Good idea." I try to act chill and like this is totally normal, but it's hard to tell if I'm pulling it off, because on the inside I'm jumping up and down and screaming. Also, I can't tell if he's talking super quietly because he's nervous or because he doesn't want Kyle to hear him.

"All right. Good. That's good." He nods. "I wasn't sure. I mean, never mind." Tate takes a deep breath like he's relieved. Like he was worried there was a chance I'd say no. He walks around the table and slides his phone into my hand, because we aren't supposed to have our phones on at school. It's warm like he's been holding it all day, and by the transitive property, it's kind of like our hands are touching. I type in my number and save it as "Rachel Brooks" in case he knows another Rachel.

"Did I tell you we won our first game?" Tate asks.

"No," I say, looking up at him. "That's awesome. How many more games do you have to win to make the play-offs?"

"Six."

"You can do it," I say.

"Thanks." He smiles at me.

I'm about to give Tate my phone so he can add his number when I see Coach Howard walking over to us. I turn off my sound, call my phone from his, and then hang up. I put my phone in my pocket and hand his back to him.

Tate leans in really close and whispers, "Good call," in my ear. Maybe he isn't trying to hide from anyone after all.

After lunch, I sneak into the bathroom and save his number as "Tate," because I don't know any other Tates.

I like the way his name looks in my phone.

My trip downtown was a disaster, but it made me realize something: I'm done with gym. I can't spend my one free hour doing yoga. I need time out of the brace that belongs to me.

I do my homework in the kitchen and wait for Dad to get home. It's quiet except for the regular sounds our house makes: the low hum of the fridge and the wind breathing and sighing outside the wall of windows. It's dark by the time I hear the garage door and the sound of Dad's heavy dress shoes clapping against the wood stairs. "Hello," he says, like he's surprised to see me waiting for him. "Where's your mother?"

"I think she's sleeping," I say.

"I guess it's almost ten." Dad sighs. "Anything good for dinner?"

I shrug.

"Salmon?" he asks.

I nod. "It's not bad," I say.

"Mm-hmm." Dad smiles and walks over to the fridge. He takes out the plate of food Mom made for him and puts it in the microwave. "How's school?"

"It's okay." I should wait a little longer before asking him for something. "It's a little harder than last year. But not that much."

"Good," he says.

"Hey, Dad?"

"Yes?"

The air feels thick and I'm scared he'll say no or "Ask your mother" before I even finish. "I was wondering if, um . . . You know how you wrote me that note so I wouldn't have to go to gym?"

"I know I have a lot of gray hair, but I'm not senile yet." He smiles at me.

I smile back. Dad is in one of his silly moods. "I was

wondering if you could write it for the rest of the year. I want to have an hour every day where I can do whatever I want. I think it would really help me."

The microwave goes off—BEEP, BEEP, BEEP. They're the longest, loudest beeps in the history of the world. Dad takes out his food and slams the door shut. He walks over to the silverware drawer, grabs a fork and knife, and sits down next to me at the table. He takes off his tie, and I'm pretty sure he's about to give me his answer when Mom walks into the kitchen. "Hi, honey. Did you find dinner?" Pillow lines criss-cross her face and her eyes are half-closed, but her blonde bob is still perfect.

"I did." Dad stands up and gives her a kiss. "It looks delicious."

Mom rolls her eyes because even she knows he's lying. His dinner is healthy and overcooked. It's steamed cardboard.

"Rachel," Dad says, turning back around like nothing could distract him from answering me. "You are playing soccer every day. When does that end?"

"It doesn't. I'm playing indoor, and then spring soccer."

"As long as you're getting regular exercise and making time to stretch out of the brace, I don't see why not. I'll write you a note for the next few months."

"Thank you!" I say.

"You don't see why not what?" Mom asks.

No, Mom, please don't screw this up for me.

"Rachel doesn't want to go to gym anymore," Dad says.

"Why not?" Mom asks, like she's about to overrule him.

I take a deep breath. I try to stay calm and explain myself. "I want to have one hour a day I can look forward to without my brace."

The kitchen is silent. No one says anything. Dad is waiting for Mom, and Mom is going to say no.

She opens her mouth like she's about to say something and then doesn't. She throws her hands in the air. "I went to gym," she says. Then she walks out of the kitchen.

Dad sighs. "You didn't do anything wrong. I'm glad you told us what you needed. It's just—it's hard for Mom."

He takes out his prescription pad and writes a note excusing me from gym. And now, because I asked for it, I have an hour that's all mine.

thirteen

THE NEXT DAY at practice, Hazel shows up two minutes late with Ladan. They stand off to the side during warm-ups and whisper to each other.

"Let's pair off. One person from each group, go grab a ball," Coach Howard says. "We're going to work on agility before we jump into passing drills."

I jog over to the balls and so does Hazel. "Ready?" I ask her.

"Oh, um, I actually already told Ladan I'd pass with her today. That's cool with you, right? I mean, she asked me first, so . . ."

"Oh. Yeah. Okay." I nod. I know if I say, "No, it's really not okay," I'll sound crazy. So I will not make it into a thing, or about me, because it's probably not.

"Cool." Hazel smiles at me and then dribbles away.

"Do you have a partner?" I ask Frannie when she runs over to grab a ball.

"What do you mean?" She looks confused. "Where's Hazel?"

I shrug.

"Ignore her." Frannie rolls her eyes. "She's being weird today."

"You think?" I ask.

"Yeah," she says.

"Good. I thought it was just me."

"Definitely not." Frannie smiles at me.

I smile back. "I'm thinking about trying out your idea."

"This one?" She sticks her butt out and then passes the ball to me.

I laugh. "Just like that." I try kicking the ball to her with my left foot, because I need to practice on that side. It comes up short and a little misdirected.

"I like it," she says, running forward to get the ball. She doesn't say anything or seem to mind chasing after it, so I don't switch back to my right side. I work on my left kicks until Coach Howard blows the whistle and asks us to circle up around the goal.

"We're running three-on-three drills today. Everyone is going to play both offense and defense," she announces. She splits us up into two groups and sends me to the line behind the goal.

Coach Howard blows the whistle and I run to cover Hazel. I stay close to her and shuffle backward, keeping my eyes on the ball, waiting for her to slip up or lose her balance. When she goes to pass, I take the ball and dribble out. Ladan runs over and pushes me toward the sideline, until it's almost impossible for me to dribble around her. She has me cornered, covering me on my right, because she's figured out that that's my sort of good side. I pretend like I'm about to take a chance and dribble left, and then when she goes in to take the ball from me, I lean forward and let my brace box her out. She steps back enough for me to pivot right and get around her.

I can't believe it actually works. I'm so stunned that I don't realize Ladan is in front of me again, and before I can think of what to do next, she takes the ball away from me and passes it to Hazel. Hazel taps it to Frannie, Frannie scores, and they all high-five each other.

"Good work," I say to Josie and Emily as we run back to the halfway line and wait for our chance on offense. Josie doesn't even bother to look at me, but I don't care. I spend the rest of practice running plays in my head, imagining what it will be like to use my brace to help me in a real game situation.

After practice, I'm in my room trying to understand math and listening to the Jackson 5. When "ABC" comes on, I start tapping my hands against my stomach without even realizing it. My drumming sounds pretty good, and it's really fun to find the beat and the tempo, so I keep experimenting with different patterns, moving my hands in circles and then side to side on the brace. I can't believe I have a built-in drum and it's been here this whole time. I'm so into the song and my brace drum that I almost don't notice my phone buzzing. I keep the beat going with one hand and pick up my phone with the other.

It's a text from Tate! I look again to make sure it's really him. *It is! We are officially texting!*

Do you get to pick the baby's name? It isn't even a text about science. It's about life, which is a way bigger deal.

Doubt it, I say. No one's asked for my opinion.

Rude, he writes back.

Their loss, I say. I have a lot of good ideas, like Tristan, because it's unique and strong and cool all at the same time.

Unique is overrated, he says. Trust me.

Tate is good unique, I say.

Thanks. That's nice, he says. You should just give your parents a list of all the names you like.

Good call. My back is aching inside the brace, so I move my homework and stretch out across the bed before typing the next part. Did I tell you that my mom told me it's a boy? I ask.

No way! Finally! That's awesome, he says. Got to go. Dinner.

K. Bye, I say.

Bye, he says.

I read our conversation over a few times before bed. Even though falling asleep in the brace is sometimes hard, it's not as bad when the boy you like texted you.

The next day, I make a list of my favorite baby names like Tate suggested. I'm planning to leave it on Mom's nightstand, but I decide I should sleep on it for a few nights or weeks or however long it takes to be sure I'm giving Mom and Dad my best and most creative ideas, because this is a really, really important decision.

RACHEL'S TOP FIVE BABY NAMES

(in order of importance)

1. TRISTAN
2. DANIEL
3. CONNOR
4. KAI
5. MATEO

~

My new "stick-my-butt-out technique" in soccer is not foolproof or magical or anything, but I've been playing better ever since I started using it. By our fourth game, I haven't come in contact with any other fakers. The only issue is that Coach Howard doesn't seem to notice I'm improving. I was only on the field for ten minutes in the last game and thirteen in the one before that, and in both games, she divided up my playing time, probably so I wouldn't be able to tell that I wasn't on the field for very long or feel as bad about it. I noticed, but I stayed focused and guarded my side of the field. I didn't mess anything up in either game. I even had a big play where I cleared the ball from the goal. It felt good to play like that again, like someone who could make a difference for the team.

The other good thing that happened last week was that I figured out how to put the brace on by myself. I went straight to the locker room after school and took it off to stretch out before practice. Hazel has always helped me put the brace back on after I'm done, but she never showed up. She went down to the field with Ladan and forgot to tell me. By the time I realized that she wasn't coming, I only had five minutes to get to practice, and I couldn't ask anyone else for help, because there was no one left in the locker room.

It took me a few tries to figure out that when I put the brace on myself I need to start by buckling on the middle strap and pull really hard. And now I don't need help getting it on or off. I don't know why it took me so long to try. I guess when you don't have another choice, you have to make things happen for yourself, or they won't.

fourteen

HALLOWEEN IS TWO weeks away, but no one has mentioned dressing up or trick-or-treating to me. I guess it seems a little babyish, which is weird because this time last year, Frannie, Hazel, and I had our roller-girl costumes planned and our candy route mapped out. Literally. But now that we're in seventh grade, we're supposed to be too cool and mature to care.

I do care, though. Halloween is our thing. I'd love to use my free hour to get dressed up in matching outfits and go around to different houses. I wouldn't be able to binge on all the candy, but that wouldn't be too bad. Eating in the brace is a lot easier now that I've learned when to stop, and I could probably eat a few pieces between houses and still have time to digest.

"Are we trick-or-treating this year?" I ask Frannie and Hazel at lunch.

Hazel gives Frannie a look I've never seen before. I don't know what it means, but as soon as it happens, I realize how weird it is that I'm the one bringing this up. Costumes are Frannie's territory, so I'm never the person who decides what we're doing or wearing. And it seems really weird that the soccer team isn't planning anything.

"I'm surprised you'd even want to get dressed up." The way Hazel's voice swings up and down makes it obvious that she memorized this line. She would be a terrible actress.

"It would be fun," I say. "Remember, we talked about wearing the grass skirts as part of our costumes?"

There's the look again, passing between them. This time, I know for sure I'm on the outside of something.

"What?" I ask.

"I told you," Hazel says. "We didn't think you'd want to get dressed up this year because, you know." She glances down at my brace. "And it's too late to get another ticket now."

"A ticket to what?" I ask.

"The haunted house at Andover High." She picks up a baby carrot and pops it in her mouth. "It's sold out. I guess it's really popular this year, since Halloween is on a Friday."

"When did you decide to go?" I ask.

"Last week," Hazel says. "Ladan asked some peeps from the team about going together. I told her I didn't think you'd want to go because it'd be longer than an hour."

"You did?" Frannie asks.

My cheeks are burning, probably red and splotchy by now—a dead giveaway that I'm hurt. They made a whole plan for Halloween and didn't tell me. Best friends are supposed to share everything, not leave each other out of costumes and haunted houses. "Maybe I could still get a ticket?" My words taste desperate.

"Doubt it," Hazel says. "I mean, you can check. I'm not lying about them being sold out."

I keep waiting for her to realize how mean she sounds. I wonder if she knows, because I think that might be worse. I don't call her out on it, because there's a chance that if I open my mouth everything I'm feeling will pour out of me, and I don't want to say anything to Hazel that I can't take back.

"I don't have to go," Frannie says to me. "I don't even want to. No one else actually cares about dressing up anyway. They all want to look cute. I'm sorry, but you can't be a witch without at least one wart, and a tight black dress is not authentic. It's not practical for flying around on a broom. Everyone knows that."

"You can't leave me alone," Hazel says to Frannie.

"You'll be with the other girls," she says. "Rachel, we can get dressed up for real and go all out. I have a million ideas."

"Where would you even go?" Hazel asks before I have a chance to respond.

"Trick-or-treating!" I say.

"Yes!" Frannie says.

"That could be cool too." Hazel plays with her hair.

"It will be." Frannie smiles at me.

"I'll map out a new candy route," I say.

"Perfect!" Frannie says. "This is going to be awesome."

I love her for trying to make it better, for picking me over everyone else. It helps.

fifteen

I WALK OUT onto the field in my uniform with the rest of the team. I wish I'd told Mom not to come to this game and that I hardly play anymore, but I completely forgot, so she's here, folding chair and all. "Go, Rachel!" She smiles and waves to me. It feels like she's mocking me.

Coach Howard puts me in on defense about halfway through the first half. I can't let anyone get through to the goal. If we win the next two games, we get to go to the playoffs, and even though I'm not starting or playing very much, I still want our team to win.

I cover the girl in red who's carrying the ball up the left side of the field. She tries to fake me out, dragging the ball to the side. I don't fall for it. I stay with her and wait for my chance to get the ball as she inches her way toward our goal. She taps the ball between my legs and sprints around me before I can stop her. I run to catch up with her, but she pings the ball to her teammate, and they score the first goal of the game. The red team erupts. They're all shouting and cheering for each other.

Coach Howard pulls me off the field. No one says, "Good work" or, "Way to hustle out there" or anything to me. They whisper things to each other, and I stare at the grass. I wish I could blame it on the brace, but what happened was all me.

No one else scores for the rest of the game.

"Good try today, honey," Mom says to me when we get in the car.

"You're not serious," I say.

"Yes, I am. I think it's good that you're out there giving it your all."

"Nothing about today was good."

"You're being too hard on yourself."

"Stop. We're not going to the play-offs because of me." I say it a little too loudly.

"Don't yell at me," Mom shouts back.

It feels like we're always fighting or almost fighting. It used to be like this every six months when we went to see Dr. Paul, and now every six months is every day.

sixteen

ON HALLOWEEN, FRANNIE'S dad picks the three of us up from school. Hazel is going to the haunted house with the soccer girls and Frannie and I are going trick-or-treating, but we're all getting ready together.

Practice was canceled because it's been raining all day, which is good because even if no one is talking about how I let in the one and only goal at the game two days ago, I know they're all still thinking about it, because I am. My shoes make a squishy sound when I climb into the backseat. Everything I'm wearing feels wet. I thought ahead and stashed a second outfit in my bag in case I get uncomfortable and my brace starts pulling on my clothes in a weird way, which happens sometimes. Even if I never change, knowing the option is there makes me feel better.

As soon as we get to Frannie's house, I change out of my school clothes and into a long baby-doll shirt and the new leggings Mom bought me. The leggings are my favorite things to wear, because they're thin but still warm, and they have this special grip on the inside so they don't move around under the brace. They've pretty much solved the pants problem. I don't think I've ever worn this exact outfit to school, but I like it a lot and I could. I feel pretty and it's comfortable, which is a dream combo. Plus, my hair is a little wavy from the rain. It looks like I spent all day at the beach.

Frannie and Hazel are sitting on the carpet sorting through enormous piles of costumes when I get upstairs. "Everything is curated by decade and/or genre," Frannie says as I drop down next to them.

Hazel rolls her eyes at me. "Curate" is Frannie's new favorite word.

"I wish I were going with you guys," Hazel says. I try not to let her comment bother me, but it does a little. "I'd be very into eating pounds of chocolate right now."

"When would you not be into that?" Frannie asks.

"Good point." Hazel smiles.

I hear the muffled sound of tiny bells. Everyone who texts me is currently in the room, which means it has to be Tate. I roll over onto my hands and knees and push myself up as fast as I can. I don't usually get up that way in front of other people, but at this point, I'm not hiding anything from my friends. I unzip the front pocket of my backpack. His name makes me smile.

Going to the haunted house tonight?

Sold out, I write back, then Frannie and I are trick-or-treating. What are you up to? I press send and then re-read what I wrote a few times. I wish I'd sent it all in one text, so it would take up less space on my screen and my words wouldn't seem so much bigger than his. I want it to feel like we are trying the same amount, but he is trying a little more because he texted me first.

He doesn't write back for four minutes. It makes me think I should have waited to write back too. Finally he says, I want to trick-or-treat! But Kyle said we're too old.

I laugh. Haha! No way! You're never too old for unlimited candy.

"Who's that?" Hazel asks.

"Tate," I say before I can stop myself.

"Wait, what? That's amazing!" she squeals. "Texting is one step away from going out. Trust me."

I want to believe her. I hear the bells again, sparkling from inside my glittery turquoise case. I have an extra ticket, he says. Meet in front at 8?

"Fran, want to go with Hazel tonight?" I ask, because I'm not ditching her. "Tate has an extra ticket. But if you'd still rather trick-or-treat, I'm totally good with that too."

"I know I have something for three people," Frannie says to herself, digging around in the pile in front of her. "Sorry, Hazel, but you're not being a lame witch with the soccer girls anymore."

"Whatever," Hazel says. "You're in charge."

"Is that a yes?" I ask Frannie.

"Yes!" she says.

See you at 8, I write.

Sounds good, he writes back.

"We need a costume that will work with my brace," I say. I know we'll be at the haunted house for more than an hour.

"You can't wear it tonight," Hazel says. "Tate is going to be there."

"I have to," I say.

"There's no way your mom will ever find out that you didn't wear it. It's not like it has a tracking device."

"It doesn't have to do with my mom," I say.

"Then what's the problem?"

"I can't skip hours."

"It's *one night*. It won't make a difference."

"It could," I say.

"There's no way," she says. "They're probably telling you that to scare you so you actually wear it. I bet a lot of people don't follow the rules. I mean, think about it, there has to be some cushion."

"Maybe," I say. "It's not like I want to wear my brace tonight. But if I start taking it off whenever Tate's around or whenever I don't feel like dealing with it, the hours will add up really fast, and then it might not work." As soon as I say it, I realize why Mom made such a big deal out of ten minutes. If I think ten minutes here and there doesn't matter, I won't wear it as much as I should, and I don't really know how big of a cushion I have. No one does.

"Oh. Sure. I mean, that makes sense," Hazel says. Only it doesn't seem like she really gets it.

"I've got it!" Frannie pops out from under her bed holding two long fishtails. "Mermaids! And you can be a clamshell! It'll blend right in with your brace. It's from when Lucy was in band for *The Little Mermaid* musical."

"I don't know," I say. I don't love the idea of being a bedazzled clam. But it's too late to stop Frannie. She's handing me light gray tights and a sparkling shift dress, and I guess it's probably the best option. The hard, shimmering shell that attaches to my back blends in perfectly with the brace.

When I see Tate standing in front of the haunted house in his FC Barcelona jersey and all his soccer gear, waiting for me like he said he would, I can't think about anything else.

"Sweet costumes!" Kyle shouts at us from under his gorilla mask.

"Thanks!" Hazel clings to his side. "You really think so?"

"Nope. Not really."

"Shut up! You're so mean." She hits his shoulder, not like she wants it to hurt, but like she's trying to find an excuse to touch him.

"What are you supposed to be?" Kyle points at me.

I accidentally look at Tate, but he's looking at Kyle. "*He* doesn't know the answer," Kyle says. "Do you, bro?" I feel my face heat up and turn red.

"Yeah, I do," Tate says. "They're characters from that movie. The one where they're all, um, under the sea. You know, the cartoon." Then he looks at the ground, like he's embarrassed. Maybe he was expecting a different version of me to show up.

"Solid guess." Kyle laughs. Then he looks at me. "Spit it out already."

"He's right. We're from *The Little Mermaid*. I'm a clam." I mumble the last part.

"Hmm." He smirks. "Weird costume."

I think about telling him to shut up, but I don't totally disagree about my costume being weird, so I change the subject instead. "Scale of one to ten, how scary is this haunted house going to be?"

"I hope ten," Frannie says. "But probably two."

"Five," Hazel says.

"Um, one," Kyle says. "It's all fake."

Tate shrugs. "No clue."

We follow the signs, which say "WATCH OUT: Satan is loose in Salem" and "BEWARE. This House is Haunted" until we are standing on the football field. There isn't much of a line to get into the long tent, but once we're on the other side of the heavy curtains, it's dark and crowded. The music sounds very *dun-dun-dun*, like something bad and scary is about to happen, and I can't see anything other than hands and eyes popping out at me. Someone pushes against me like they're trying to knock me down, and the grass is wet. I slip backward and land in a cold, slimy puddle.

"Kyle!" I hear Hazel shriek. "Where are you?" She's way ahead of me.

"Coming." His voice is close. He's standing right next to me.

I try to push myself up with both hands and lean to the right, because even though I'm not as strong on that side, nothing is digging into my armpit and my hip is free to help. But my hand slips and slides under me, and I end up falling back into the mud. "Hey, what the—" someone shouts. "You can't sit down in the middle of the path. People are trying to get by."

"Because obviously that's what I'm doing," I shout back.

"Rachel?" Tate says.

No! "Yeah." My voice is so soft I almost can't hear it.

"Why are you sitting down?"

"I fell," I say.

"Do you, um, need help?"

"Uh, yeah." I reach out and feel my way around in the air until I find one of Tate's hands. He grabs on to me and pulls me up. All I can think about is that his skin is touching mine, and then I lose my grip and fall backward onto the ground again. *Plop.* So does Tate. *Plop.*

"So . . . that didn't go very well." Tate starts laughing.

I start laughing too.

"Do you think you can get up on your own?" he asks. "Or should we try that again? I'm down for whatever."

"I think I can do this."

"Okay," he says. "I'm standing by just in case."

I do the only thing I know will definitely work: I roll onto my knees and push myself up with both hands. I don't care if his eyes have adjusted to the dark and he can see me. He's doing everything he can to help me and acting like he doesn't care about my brace, so why should I? "Okay. I'm ready."

He grabs my muddy hand and leads me back outside. I'm covered in mud, and so is Tate.

"Thanks for helping me," I say.

"A for effort?"

"Definitely." I nod. "You can go back in if you want. You didn't get to see any of the haunted house."

He shakes his head. "Don't tell Kyle, but I hate haunted houses."

"We should have gone trick-or-treating," I say.

"I'd have an entire bucket of Snickers by now, and we wouldn't look like—"

We both laugh.

"Is your, um, is it okay? Your brace?" he asks.

"I mean, mud wrestling isn't recommended, but it'll be fine."

"Cool." He pushes back his hair. "I wasn't sure if it could get wet."

"Well, I'm not supposed to go swimming or shower in it, but it doesn't feel wet inside, so I think I'm okay."

"Good." He smiles, and right now, my brace doesn't feel like something I have to hide.

Kyle and Hazel come out of the haunted house holding hands, followed by Frannie and most of the girls' soccer team. They're all dressed sort of like witches: tight black clothes, pointy hats, and brooms. It's more witch-inspired.

"Dude," Kyle says as soon as he sees Tate. "What happened to you?"

"I fell," Tate says, covering for me. I can't help but smile.

"Since when do you fall? Other than never."

"It was dark in there," Tate says. Then he looks at me, and our eyes stay glued together. I know he doesn't care about Kyle or being covered in mud, and I don't either.

"Dude, did she take you down?" Kyle points at me.

"Actually, someone pushed me, and Tate was trying to help," I say. Kyle already knows that, since he's the one who did the pushing. But I can't say that part out loud, because Hazel is holding his hand and leaning into him.

"Just like she's dragging down the soccer team," Josie says partly under her breath, but loud enough for everyone to hear. Someone gasps, and a few of the girls smirk or cover their mouths, pretending like they're trying not to laugh.

I swallow hard, but Frannie says, "Wait, remind me who was playing goalie again?"

“It was my first time!” Josie says.

“Sweet excuse.” Frannie rolls her eyes.

I love her for backing me up and being my ally always. And I want to think Josie is wrong and stupid and just ignore her. But I know she’s right. We lost because of me.

seventeen

I WAKE UP way too early on Saturday morning. Eight a.m. too early. All I want to do is fall back asleep and not think about the game or what Josie said, but I can't stop my brain from showing the instant replay.

Two hours later, I can't take it anymore. I know there's a chance Frannie is still sleeping. Out of the three of us, she sleeps the latest. But I decide it's worth the risk. I get dressed and walk over to her house. She answers the door, eyes half-open, like she could fall back asleep standing there.

"You're lucky my dad already woke me up." She fake glares at me. "Want breakfast? He made pancakes."

I shake my head. "I need your help," I say. "I'm bad at soccer."

"You're not that—"

"I am." I don't let her lie to me. "The brace is holding me

back and I don't know what to do. The secret-weapon-butt technique is good, but there aren't enough situations where I can use it. I need something else. And I can't do this alone."

She nods. "We need water bottles and oranges. Meet at your house in ten?"

I nod back. "Thank you."

"Always," she says.

Ten minutes later, we're warming up in my backyard. "You're not going to like what I'm about to say," Frannie says between toe taps on the ball.

"Nothing could be worse than what Josie said last night."

"Ignore her."

"She's right," I say.

"She's a follower," Frannie says. "But listen, you want the truth?"

"Yes."

"I really don't think you're going to get to play offense. You have to take what you can get."

"Defense," I say.

"Exactly. And there are a lot of good parts about playing defense. I get that it feels not as important sometimes, because you're not scoring, but you know what happens when the defense goes wrong."

"Um, yeah, what happened at our last game," I say. I know she's right, and that she's not trying to make me feel bad. "Okay." I nod. "I'm ready."

We run one-on-one drills. After about twenty minutes, it's Frannie's turn with the ball. I see my chance to break in, but she runs around me and scores.

"UGH," I shout. I feel like I have no control over my body. I sit down on the grass. It hasn't dried out from the rain, and now my butt is wet.

Frannie walks over and sits next to me. "Ooo," she says, but she doesn't get up.

"Should I give up?" I ask her.

She shrugs. "If you want to."

That's not what I'm expecting or what I want to hear. I can't imagine it: my life without soccer. I've been playing every fall and spring since second grade. And last year, I started playing indoor soccer too, because I didn't like how the winter felt without the team or my friends or the game. "Would you give up?" I ask. "If you were wearing a brace? And if Josie said all that stuff about you?"

"I want to say no, but I have no idea." She shakes her head. "I really don't."

"That's fair," I say. "You know, my mom didn't even think I should try to play anymore."

"What? That doesn't sound like something your mom would say."

"She's been so weird about everything with the brace. We never talk about it, and when we do, it's only because she's reminding me that I need to follow every single rule perfectly."

"That must make it so much harder. I mean, not talking always makes everything a lot worse for me."

"Really?" I ask.

"Yeah. Sometimes with my dad, we just won't talk for days about anything other than dinner, and those stretches are always the worst."

"Same!" I say. "But I'm so mad at her for acting like wearing a brace is no big deal. I don't even *want* to talk to her about it. Ever."

"You should tell her she's making it worse," Frannie says.

"I don't think she'll listen to me. I mean, she had a brace, so she knows what I'm going through. But she acts like I'm just supposed to deal with it and have no feelings about it because it's not as bad as her surgery."

"You're allowed to have feelings, especially about your own brace. Trust me," she says. "Dad, Lucy, and me—we're all in so much pain about Mom, sometimes it's like we can't even deal. But it's always worse when we don't talk about it, because we all need different things. My dad says it's my job to tell him what I need, because he can't guess and he doesn't want to try. I think you should take that advice with your mom, because not telling her is getting in the way. She probably doesn't even realize how annoying she's being. I mean, she can't read your mind. No one can."

"True," I say. "I don't even know where to start. She gets defensive about every little thing."

"Maybe ask her to listen to you," she says. "Start there."

"That's a really good idea."

We sit in silence for a few minutes, and then Frannie says, "What do you want to do about soccer?"

I think about it. "I want to give up. I'm sick of being bad. But if I didn't play, I wouldn't get to hang out with you and Hazel as much, and I have no idea what I'd do after school other than listen to music and sit around thinking about how much I wish I didn't have to wear a brace."

She laughs.

I laugh too. It feels good to say it out loud.

I keep thinking about the things I'd miss about soccer: playing hard and fighting to get better and being part of a team. Every time I take my place on the field, I feel this rush of energy pumping through me, filling me with excitement and happiness and hope that I can do anything. I know I can be good at soccer, even in the brace. I can be someone the team can rely on to help win games, and I want to prove I'm right about that. I roll over and push myself off the ground. "Let's go," I say to Frannie.

"Really?" she asks.

"Yes," I say.

"I was hoping you'd say that. I would totally get it if you decided you didn't want to play anymore, but I'd miss hanging out with you every day."

"Me too," I say.

She stands up. "Okay, so, I think you need to give up on your left leg for now. It's fine for dribbling, but you don't have enough flexibility in that hip to be able to kick or pass. You need to get to the point where your right leg is dominant. Basically, you have to turn yourself into a righty."

"That's impossible," I say.

She shakes her head. "You just have to practice a lot."

"I don't have a choice, do I?"

"No. Not really," she says. "But if you can make this happen, after you get your brace off, you'll have two dominant legs. You'll be unstoppable."

I nod. "Okay, so what's the plan?"

"Drills."

I practice passing and pinging and kicking the ball to Frannie over and over with my right foot for the next few hours, until it starts to feel natural.

Mom makes fettuccini and meatballs with red sauce for dinner, which is my all-time favorite food after pizza, and as soon as I sit down at the table, she says, "I want to talk to you about something—"

"Okay." I stack a few meatballs on my pasta and drown them in marinara. Then I sprinkle a thick layer of Parmesan on top.

"I know we talked about it before, but I want to say it again just in case. Things are going to start to change around here after the baby is born, and I want to make sure you feel like you can ask me questions or talk to me if you're worried about anything."

"Okay," I say. "I don't have any right now, but I'll let you know if that changes."

"That sounds good," Mom says.

"I made a list of names I like," I say. I stand up and walk over to my backpack. I unzip the front pocket and pull out the folded piece of paper. I haven't changed anything since I first made the list, but I read through it one last time before I hand it to Mom.

She looks it over and smiles. "You probably won't believe this, but we have a lot of the same favorites."

She's right. It surprises me that we agree on anything anymore.

eighteen

ON MONDAY, I'M nervous for the last game of the fall season, but I'm excited too. Frannie and I practiced again on Sunday, and I'm getting better and more confident at kicking with my right leg. For the first time in forever, it feels like there's a chance I could actually play well. I'm glad I asked Frannie for help.

The thermometer on our kitchen window says thirty-seven degrees, so I pack a long-sleeved shirt and leggings to wear under my uniform. I grab a Snickers bar for Tate from the leftover Halloween candy Mom bought. I know it's very boyfriend/girlfriend to give each other things, and I'm not sure exactly where we stand after what happened at the haunted house, but I'm pretty sure he like-likes me too. I don't know if he wants to be BF/GF, though, because that's a whole different official level I've never experienced before. I'm not even sure how you can tell if someone wants to be your boyfriend. But if I had to guess, I'd say he probably tries to help you with things like getting out of the mud, and he also probably doesn't care about things like the fact that you have a back brace. I mean, no one really makes a big deal about my brace or stares at me anymore. Everyone knows, and I guess they're all used to it by now. But Tate acts like it doesn't matter to him at all. And that makes me like him even more.

The good news about the sudden drop in temperature is that the brace with all its extra padding actually keeps me super warm, which means I can dress like I always do and feel toasty. I almost feel bad for all the non-brace wearers, aka everyone else at school, because they need to pile on extra layers today and I don't.

At school, everyone is in the lobby before class starts, waiting for the bell to ring, because it's too cold to stand outside. The air is thick and sweaty. Lucky for me, Hazel and Frannie are standing right near the door, so I don't have to push through the crowd to get to them. "I can't believe we have to play Hill today," Hazel says. "It's freezing outside. I mean, come on."

"I can't wait," I say.

"Did I miss something?" Hazel looks at Frannie like, *What planet is she living on?*

"Just wait." Frannie smiles at her.

"Sneaky." Hazel crosses her arms. "I like it."

I want to tell her what Frannie and I have been up to, but

I don't want to jinx my luck. "Does anyone else think it smells like an armpit in here?" I ask.

"Seriously. Deodorant. Get some, people!" Frannie shouts. "The nurse is giving it away for free."

"Thanks for the tip," Tate says. I look up as soon as I hear his voice. "Hey, um, Rachel, can I talk to you?" He pushes his hair back, and all I can think about is what Hazel said about texting being one step away from going out.

"Um. Yeah. Sure." I flip my hair too. I try to act totally and completely chill, even though my heart feels like it's actually about to escape from my chest. I meet Hazel's eyes, and she mouths, "OMG! It's happening!"

I smile at her.

I follow Tate's bright green sneakers away from my friends until he stops walking. "I was wondering if—" He pauses. "I came to ask—"

It feels like whatever is making Tate nervous is rubbing off on me, because out of nowhere I'm queasy and hot under not-that-many layers.

"So, um, Kyle wants to know if Hazel would maybe want to go out with him," he says in a rush.

It feels like all the blood is being drained from my body. "Sure," I say and walk back to Hazel. "Tate wants to know if you want to go out with Kyle." I try not to look directly at her when I say it. I don't want to see her smile, because even though I know she's not gloating, that's how it will feel.

"YES!" Hazel shrieks. "Tell him yes!" She's nodding her head so hard and fast I'm afraid it might fall off.

I walk back over to Tate.

"I heard," he says.

"I'm pretty sure Kyle heard," I say under my breath.

He smiles and then turns to walk away.

"Tate," I say, and he turns back around. I take off my backpack and pull the Snickers out of the front pocket. "Because you didn't get to go trick-or-treating."

He smiles wider. "Thanks, Rachel. You remembered. That's really cool." He slips it into his back pocket and then walks over to Kyle.

Hazel is squealing. "I can't believe it! Kyle is my boyfriend. I have a boyfriend. That makes us the fifth new couple in our grade this year."

I am happy for Hazel, and I don't want to be jealous. I hate that I am. I know it's not her fault that it wasn't me. I smile as big as I can at her, until my face starts to ache as much as everything else.

I go to the soccer field early to stretch out and warm up before everyone else arrives. Only, when I get there, Hazel and Frannie are already there with the forwards. They're sitting in a circle talking and stretching.

"Rachel." Hazel sounds surprised. "You're here. Sit. We're talking seventh grade formal."

"I can't believe it's only five weeks away," Ladan says.

"Seriously." Hazel nods.

"We're in charge of decorations." Frannie looks at Hazel and then at me. "I signed all three of us up. I'm not going to a dance with a dumb theme. Last year it was ridiculous. I mean, hearts? Really? That's not a theme. It's like they didn't even try."

"I guess that's one good thing about not making the playoffs. More time for decorating." Ladan looks at me when she says it, so I know she thinks that it's my fault we didn't make it. It stings behind my eyes, but I don't even try to defend myself, because Ladan is the best player on the team and everything she says sounds like a fact.

"With Frannie, there's always time for decorating," Hazel says.

"What are you wearing?" Ladan is still looking at me, but it's one of those general questions that anyone could answer, so I pretend not to hear her. I don't want to think about going to the dance in my brace.

"I'm wearing red," Frannie says.

"You're so lucky." Ladan rubs cherry gloss onto her already shimmery lips. "My mom won't let me wear red until I'm like eighteen or married or something stupid. She's so strict. It's a Persian thing."

"Red is *très chic*. You should tell her I said so." Frannie pretends it's no big deal that her mom isn't here to have an opinion on the color of her dress.

"Rachel found this purple dress that's totally gorge!" Hazel says out of nowhere. I get that she's trying to move the conversation away from Frannie and her mom, and I can't blame her for that, but I don't have a dress for the dance. I tried on a dress that Hazel and I both loved when we went to the mall together over the summer, but I didn't buy it and she knows I can't wear anything like it anymore.

"What's it like?" Ladan asks me.

I don't know what to say, and I'm afraid nothing is going to come out right. "It's hard to describe."

"It's not. No one's going to think you're being braggy, Rachel," Hazel says. "It has a sweetheart neckline." She runs the tips of her fingers over her chest like she's drawing it.

"I'm not sure I'm getting that one anymore," I say. "I mean, I think I found something even cuter." The words fall out of my mouth, jumbling together in the air. I hope they don't sound too much like a lie.

"I love it," Ladan says. "So many options. I seriously can't wait."

I can. I wish I hadn't told Hazel and Frannie I'd go with them way back when we first found out about the seventh grade formal. It feels like a promise, like something I can't take back. I mean, what am I supposed to do if Tate actually asks me to dance? I can't. *Plastic. Hips.* He'll probably end up dancing with someone normal, and I'll have to stand in the corner and watch the whole thing.

Sometimes, like right now, for example, I wonder what it would be like if I knew someone else who had a brace, besides Mom. I could ask her what she thinks about things like dances and dresses and boys.

"I can't wear anything like that dress anymore," I whisper to Hazel as we walk onto the field.

"Oh. I didn't realize." She puts her hand over her mouth. "I mean, it's a special occasion. I assumed you wouldn't have to wear the brace."

"I always have to wear it," I say. "There are no special occasions."

"I just thought—"

I shake my head.

"I'm sorry. That's so not fair."

"It's fine," I say, even though I'm sick of being the one with the problem, and I'm pretty sure she's sick of it too.

Between warm-ups and the huddle, I walk over to Coach Howard. She glances up from her clipboard. "Hi, Rachel," she says.

"I'm really ready for today," I say. "Frannie and I ran drills all weekend."

"I'm so glad to hear you're feeling more confident." Coach Howard smiles at me, and it's not some fake, see-through adult smile either.

"I'm sorry about the last game. I know I lost it for us—and the play-offs."

"One person can't lose a game," she says. "It takes the whole team to do that."

I want to believe her, but I keep thinking about what Ladan said earlier and what Josie said at the haunted house and how most of the team laughed like they agreed with her. "It's okay." I shrug. "I know it's my fault."

"Rachel, I've been coaching soccer for three years and I've played my whole life. I've lost a lot of games, and I promise it's never because of one person." She rests her hand on my shoulder. "I don't blame you for what happened at our game, and I'd really hate to see you take responsibility for something that wasn't your fault."

"You really don't think it was my fault?" I ask, because it surprises me.

"I wouldn't say something that wasn't true to make you feel better." She smiles.

I nod and try to let her words sink in, because now I know she means everything she said. She doesn't think we lost because of me.

"I think you've been hard on yourself, when things are already harder for you right now. I'd like you to give yourself credit for the work you've put in and the progress you've made. You've really pushed yourself, and I've noticed."

"Thanks." I grin. She sees how hard I'm working to get better. And that makes me want to keep trying.

"Get out there and have fun today," she says.

That's exactly what I do. About three quarters of the way through the first half, Coach Howard puts me in for Josie. Josie rolls her eyes at me when she jogs off the field and doesn't even give me a low five when I put my hand out, which, by the way, is pretty much standard protocol. Rude. Just rude. But whatever. I don't have time for haters. I keep moving on the balls of my feet even when nothing is happening on my side of the field.

A girl in purple zigzags toward our goal. Hazel has her covered. I sprint toward the nearest open player. She's fast, but I stay on her. When the girl Hazel is guarding passes the ball to my player, I get in the way, and without thinking, I ping the ball to Emily, one of our midfielders, with my right foot, just like I practiced with Frannie. It flies above the grass and lands at Emily's feet.

Coach Howard doesn't take me out for the rest of the half. And then the best thing ever happens: I start in the second half of the game!

I stay focused and do my best every chance I get. I only let one player get by me.

Coach Howard rotates me out toward the end of the game, which is annoying because I don't want to stop playing, but I was on the field for almost twenty minutes. It's the most I've played since I got the brace. I didn't let anyone get by me the whole game. And we win, four to zero!

Hazel's mom drops me at home afterward. Mom is sitting at the kitchen table stitching the letter "A" into the center of a hand-knit blanket. I know it's for someone else's baby because the blanket is pink, and I'm glad, because I didn't have any "A" names on my list.

I lean against the oven. It's sighing and breathing gusts of warm air. I love the way the heat feels against my chest and face. I stay there for a few extra seconds, letting my skin soak in the warmth. It reminds me of baking sugar cookies with Mom. I used to stand next to her and watch as she slid trays of our homemade treats into the oven, wishing I could be more like her.

Mom takes a deep breath, like she's about to say something important. "Can I ask how it went today?"

I nod. "Good," I say.

"I'm glad to hear your hard work over the weekend paid off."

"Thanks. It did. Coach noticed. And I think I can keep getting better."

"Of course you can." Mom says it like it's obvious to her. "Dinner will be ready soon. You must be hungry."

"Can I ask you a question?"

"You just did." I can tell Mom is smiling. She tries to twist around to face me, but with her spine, she can't move that way. "Come over here." She pats one of the empty chairs next to her, and I sit down. Her eyes have dark, tired circles around the edges. "What's going on?" she asks.

"You know how the seventh grade formal is right after Thanksgiving break?"

"Mm-hmm." She nods.

"I was wondering if maybe I could go to the dance without my brace," I say. "I'll make up the hours over the weekend."

"No," Mom says, without taking a breath or a sip of water or a second to think.

My heart stops. "Why not?"

"Because Dr. Paul said you need to wear the brace for twenty-three hours a day until you're done growing, so that's what you're going to do."

"That's not fair."

"I'm sorry." She doesn't sound sorry.

"It's three extra hours. It won't make a difference, and you know it." My voice is strained from trying not to shout.

"You don't know that. It could," she says. "It's too many hours. You won't be able to make them up."

"I will. I swear. Mom. Please."

"I really don't see how," she says. "You still have to shower and stretch every day, and you can't do either of those things in the brace."

"I can do that in ten minutes. I have before."

"You can't. It's not happening," she says. "No."

"Why not?" I ask. "Tell me the reason you won't let me."

"Because I said so," she snaps.

"Because you're trying to ruin my life!" I shout. "I can't go to the dance in my brace. I can't."

"I did! And mine was bigger!" she shouts back. "I don't understand you, Rachel. Do you want to have surgery?"

I stand up and glare at her. "Stop making everything about you!" I storm up to my room and slam the door as hard and loud as I can.

I'm doing everything I can to make sure I don't need surgery. And all I'm asking for is one night out of the brace so I can go to the formal, and have fun with my friends, and for once, not worry about stupid scoliosis.

nineteen

I'M IN THE art room the next day with Team Decorations: Frannie and Markus Steinem, who picks his nose and is probably only here to avoid being in the cafeteria at lunch. I don't get how the three of us are supposed to build a winter wonderland in five forty-five-minute lunch periods when Frannie is the only one with any artistic ability. That's the theme: "Winter Wonderland." I wish it didn't sound magical.

Today, we're sewing sparkly beads onto white fabric that will be draped around the gym. Other than the part where I'm making decorations for a dance I can't go to, I don't mind being in the art room. The walls are a mishmash of colors, covered with self-portraits of sixth, seventh, and eighth graders. It's a sea of faces looking back at me.

After thirty minutes of non-stop stitching, Frannie finally comes up for air. "Where is she?" She means Hazel.

"I have no idea," I say.

"Don't lie." Frannie's voice is huffy. "Does she seriously have someplace better to be?"

"Maybe she forgot." I don't realize the question is rhetorical until it's too late.

"That's crap, and you know it." I've never seen Frannie like this before.

"It stinks," I say, because sometimes hearing someone else say the thing you're feeling makes it easier to deal with. At least it does for me.

"Yeah." She nods. "It really does."

Hazel walks in with a few minutes left in the period. "Sorry I'm late. Kyle needed help with his math homework, and then we ended up talking for a while, you know, about us."

I wonder if she knows she's bragging and is doing it anyway, or if she just doesn't realize how into herself she sounds.

"Super fun." Frannie's words sound like spitballs.

"Everything with Kyle is fun. Or at least funny." Hazel runs her fingers along the edge of the fabric. "I can't wait for the formal! Did I tell you that Kyle and I are wearing matching outfits?" She doesn't wait for either of us to answer her question. It's a new habit she's picked up. "He's wearing this blue tie that's the exact color of my dress, so everyone will know we're boyfriend/girlfriend."

"Everyone already knows," I say. I don't look up to smile and let her in. I'm not in the mood to pretend that the fact that she ditched us to hang out with Kyle is okay when Frannie's not okay with it.

"That's exactly what Kyle said. But I want it to be obvious that we're not a regular couple. If we have matching outfits, everyone will know we're in a really, really serious relationship. You're going to feel the same way when you and Tate are boyfriend/girlfriend." She says it in this way that makes it seem like she knows everything about having a boyfriend now that she has one, and I know nothing because I don't. "By the way, I have this feeling it's going to happen at the dance. Did I tell you that already?"

I shake my head. "I'm not going to the formal," I say. I can't hold it in any longer.

"What?" Hazel asks. They both look up at me. Frannie puts down her needle.

"I can't go to the dance in my brace." I keep my voice low so Markus doesn't hear me. "I mean, I could, but I really don't want to, and I have to wear it, so I'm not going."

"Did you talk to your mom about it?" Frannie asks.

"I tried. And it didn't go very well."

"I'm sorry," she says.

"Me too," Hazel says.

"I think you should try again," Frannie says. "Or you could ask your dad?"

I nod, because I know she's right. I don't know what else to say to Mom to get her to listen to me. But Dad is a good idea.

“Am I the only one who thinks the formal is dumb?” Tate says to me in science class, while we’re supposed to be coming up with a hypothesis.

“Definitely not,” I say, even though I probably wouldn’t think it was dumb if I was going.

“Really?” he asks. “Are you going?”

I shrug, because I don’t like my answer. “Are you?” I wish he’d say no, or shrug too, so the fact that I’m not going wouldn’t feel like the end of the world.

“Kyle is making me,” he says.

“Why are you letting him do that?” I ask.

“I don’t know.” He shakes his head. “You really don’t know if you’re going?”

“I really don’t.”

“You should.” His voice is so quiet I almost miss what he says next. “It’d be more fun if you were there.”

That makes me smile. In fact, I can’t stop smiling for the rest of the day. Tate wants me to go to the dance because *I* would make it more fun for *him*. I’m pretty sure that’s boy code for he wants to be boyfriend/girlfriend.

“How was school?” Mom asks as soon as I get home.

“Fine.” I take a deep breath and follow Frannie’s advice.

"Mom, I really want to go to the dance, and I don't want to wear my brace. I promise I'll make up my hours."

"We've already talked about this. I don't want to have the same conversation again." Mom looks down at her hands. She doesn't say anything else or ask me any other questions. Obviously.

I give up and decide to wait for Dad.

By the time Dad gets home from work, Mom is already asleep, which is perfect because I don't want Mom interrupting our conversation. I've given this a lot of thought, and if Dad says I can't take my brace off for the dance, then I'll go anyway. It's really not what I want to do. But I think it would be worse for me if I stayed home by myself. I don't want to miss out on having fun with my friends and Tate because I have a brace.

The garage opens and the back door slams shut. I wait a few minutes before I walk downstairs and into the kitchen. Dad is standing by the microwave, waiting for his meal to finish re-heating.

"Hey." He takes off his tie, rolls it into a ball, and stuffs it in the pocket of his suit jacket. "Keep me company while I eat?"

I nod and sit down at the empty table.

He brings his food over and sits next to me, then looks down at his plate of pan-roasted chicken and vegetables. "Not bad."

"It's a winner," I say.

"Good. I'm hungry." He smiles at me. "How are you doing?"

I shrug. "I asked Mom if I could take my brace off for the seventh grade formal, because it's a really big deal to me, and she said I couldn't, but I thought you—"

"Might have a different answer?" he asks and then takes a bite of his dinner.

"Uh, yeah, kind of," I say. "I mean, I wasn't going to say it like that, but yeah."

"Nice try," he says. "Mom's worried. We both are. We want to make sure your brace is working before we start making concessions." He stops and looks right at me. "But I understand why you don't want to wear your brace to the formal."

"You do?" I ask.

"I know I'm your dad, but I don't live under a rock." He smiles. "It's your first big dance. Of course you want to feel your best."

"Exactly." I nod. It feels good that Dad gets it.

"Mom's not trying to make it harder for you. She just wants you to follow all the rules. It's really important to her."

"I know, and I am. But the formal is really important to me," I say. "And just so you know, I'd make up the hours. I promise."

"That's good to know," he says and nods, like it actually does matter. "Mom and I will talk about it and decide what's best for you together. I know that's not what you were hoping to hear, but it's the best I can do."

"It's good," I say. "It's better than no."

twenty

WHEN I GET to school the next day, Frannie grabs me and says, "Emergency!" She pulls me through the crowded lobby into the girls' bathroom. Hazel is in there waiting for us.

"What's going on?" I say. I'm worried Frannie texted Hazel and they had a whole back-and-forth and now I'm out of the loop about something really important. I just hope it isn't about me. "Please. Just tell me," I say to Hazel.

"I have no clue." She shrugs.

"I'm telling you both at the same exact time," Frannie says. "I heard from someone who will remain nameless, but who is a very reliable source, that there are going to be two indoor soccer teams this year. Sort of like a varsity and a JV, but apparently they're calling it the A Team and the B Team, which is obviously the exact same thing."

"No way. They can't do that," Hazel says.

"That's what's happening," Frannie says. "There isn't enough space for everyone to practice inside at the same time."

"They're picking teams." My voice comes out sounding shaky and scared. "We're going to be split up."

"That's not happening." Hazel looks at Frannie, like maybe she's as nervous as I am. "I mean, are they going to have tryouts?"

"Yeah. Monday and Tuesday after the formal," Frannie says. "We'll find out who made which team the following Monday. We need a plan. We can't be separated."

"Here's the plan: I have to make the A Team," I say.

"Me too," Hazel says.

"You had too good of a season not to make it," I say. "You and Frannie will definitely be together."

"Rachel's right," Frannie says to Hazel. "As long as you don't totally screw it up, you're on the A Team." It stings to hear Frannie say that about Hazel. If the brace hadn't happened, she might be saying the same thing about me. "I'm not going to lie to you." Frannie looks at me. "You're not even close to a shoo-in. You have to make it impossible for Coach Howard to cut you."

"What happens if that doesn't work?" Hazel says.

"We'll switch to the B—"

"No," I say before Frannie has a chance to finish. "If it doesn't work, you'll both play for the A Team, and I'll play for the B Team. No backup plan." Because even though I'm scared

I won't make the A Team, and I don't want to be alone, I can't do that to them.

I'm going to run twice as many passing, trapping, and kicking drills with my right foot for the next week. I need to do everything I can to make the A Team.

twenty-one

TWO DAYS LATER, I'm in my room doing homework and drumming along to "Cheeseburger in Paradise" when Mom knocks. She doesn't walk in without my permission, which feels like something she would have done before the brace. "Can I come in?" she asks.

"Fine," I say. This is how it's been all week: one to five words at a time.

"I—" She pauses. "I know you're upset about having to wear your *you know what* to the dance."

I hate when she talks about the brace in code, like it's a secret, when it's not.

"I came up here to tell you that Dad and I both agree with you. We think re-arranging your hours this once would be okay. So, as long as you make up the hours, you don't have to wear your brace to the dance."

I'm not sure I hear Mom right. I'm a little afraid I'm imagining her words, because I want them to be real more than anything.

"Aren't you going to say something?" she asks.

"Are you serious?" I ask.

She nods.

"Really? You promise? No takebacks?"

"I promise," she says. "We can go shopping over Thanksgiving break for a dress."

"Thank you!" I shriek. I pull myself up as fast as I can and hug her. "Thank you. Thank you. Thank you."

"You're welcome." Mom is smiling.

"From now on, do you think you could call my brace my 'brace' instead of my 'you know what'?" I ask.

"Sure." She sounds confused. "I didn't realize that bothered you."

I nod, because I'm starting to think Frannie is right—telling Mom and Dad what I need makes it better. "Thank you for listening," I say.

"Of course," she says.

"Why are you letting me do this?" I ask, because I don't understand, and I want to.

She looks down at the floor. "I was so scared that if I didn't wear my brace every second I was supposed to, they'd make me wear it for longer. Forever. Or worse, I'd need surgery. Then I did everything right and needed it anyway." She sighs.

"I'm even more scared for you, honey. I just want to make sure we do everything we can. But three hours isn't going to change the outcome. And I want you to have one night without all this responsibility." There are tears welling up in her eyes.

I reach over and hug Mom again.

She hugs me back, and she doesn't let go. I can feel her crying against my arms, and for the first time, I realize Mom is as sad for me about the brace as I am.

After Mom goes back to her room to rest, I text Hazel and Frannie, My mom changed her mind. I'm going to the dance without my brace!!!

YES! Frannie says.

Best news ever! Hazel writes. Also, I told you so. Formal is going to be HUGE for you and Tate. You're about to be the sixth new couple of the year. I know it.

Fingers crossed, I write back.

twenty-two

ON THANKSGIVING, DAD still isn't home from the hospital when Gram and Papa get to our house. Gram walks into the kitchen first. She stops to inspect Mom's antique bowls and porcelain figurines. Papa trails behind her. I can smell the turkey before I see him holding a huge aluminum-covered basin. They did some cooking this year to help Mom, since she's pregnant and can't do everything like she usually does. "Dad, let me help you," Mom says, rushing to his side.

"Thank you, Amy." Papa kisses her on the forehead and hands over the turkey. She puts it on the counter next to the pies that decorate our stovetop: apple and cranberry, Papa's favorites. "Would you look at these?" He smacks his lips.

Mom gives him a look. "I only made them because it's a holiday. You can have a sliver of each, but that's it. I need you to live forever, Dad." She grabs on to his sleeve like a little girl.

“I know, Amy.” Papa smiles and wraps his arms all the way around her. “It looks wonderful. That’s all I’m saying.”

Gram walks over to me. “Would you look at this face?” she says to everyone else, placing her fingers under my chin. Her thick Boston accent peeks through each word. “It’s really something else, and I’m not saying that because you’re my granddaughter.” Gram scans me with her light green eyes. She smiles like she’s proud, and then she looks down at the rest of me.

I stand there and wait for Gram to react. I’m used to this by now. Most people look away as fast as they can, because they don’t want me to think that they know there’s something wrong with me. Everyone else gives me the pity pout. It doesn’t bother me like it did when I first got the brace, which makes me think you really can get used to anything if you have to. But Gram’s face doesn’t give anything away. “You look beautiful,” she says. It doesn’t feel like a lie.

Papa swoops in and kisses me on the forehead, same as he did with Mom. He smells the way he always does, like new leather and aftershave.

I look back at Gram, waiting for her real reaction, but her face hasn’t changed, which means that either she loves me so much she can’t see the brace or the new dress I’m wearing looks as good as I think it does or the brace is really not a big deal. She adjusts the gold bumblebee brooch on her lapel so it doesn’t snag her cashmere sweater. Everything about my grandmother is elegant, like gold on cashmere.

Papa places his arms all the way around me. "We know how hard this whole experience is," he whispers in my ear. His voice is soft enough that Mom can't hear what he's saying. "We're very proud of you for being so strong." He takes an embroidered handkerchief from his pocket and pats it against his eyes.

I can't remember if I've ever seen Papa cry. If I have, it wasn't like this, happy and sad at the same time. I have a feeling that his tears aren't all about me—that they're about Mom too. Papa kisses me again and squeezes like he wants to protect me for as long as he can. I wish it would never end.

When he finally lets go, he looks at Mom. "How can I help?" he asks.

"You can relax," she says.

"All right. Fine. If you insist." He sits down at the table next to Gram.

We're all quiet for a minute. No one asks where Dad is. Gram and Papa know better. They're experts at filling the void Dad leaves when he's at work. I'm used to the emptiness, so I don't hate it, but I never forget it's there. And every time Dad isn't here for something big, like Thanksgiving, it feels like a knife is chipping away, making a hole inside me, and the pieces are so small there's no way to find them once they're gone.

Dad and I carve the turkey together. Always. It's our thing. He's the surgeon, and I'm chief turkey resident. We don't have that many traditions. It's mostly this and the ballet. I'm too old for dancing sugarplum fairies, but I'd rather go to *The*

Nutcracker with Dad than not. Now he's about to miss the only other thing we do together all year.

"So what else is doing?" Gram asks.

Mom and I exchange smiles, like we're passing a secret. Before this summer, whenever it was quiet in the house and we both needed to laugh, one of us would say, "So what else is doing?" like Gram. I like knowing we still have a few good things that belong to us.

"Rachel is playing so well in soccer," Mom says.

"That's wonderful," Gram says.

"I'm lucky. My friend Frannie has been coming over every day to help me get ready for tryouts, because there are two indoor teams this year, and I really want to make the A Team."

"That *is* lucky." Gram takes my hand and holds on to it.

"What time are we eating?" Papa asks.

Mom looks at the clock and takes a deep breath. "I was thinking we'd sit down in about forty-five minutes, but let's see what time David gets home." Dad was supposed to be home fourteen minutes ago. He could be stuck in traffic or stopping for gas, or he could be dealing with something bigger that will keep him away all night. Mom isn't going to call him to find out. She doesn't like to bother him when he's at work. She told me it's because she decided to marry a doctor, so she picked this life. (I didn't have a choice.)

It feels like there's a vacuum ready to suck out everything

good about this day, and we're all sitting here waiting for someone to flip the ON switch.

The phone rings.

Flip.

"Hello?" Mom answers, like she's really asking who it is, which is annoying because she already knows. "Rachel," she says. "It's for you." I feel my heart deflate inside my chest. Mom shakes her head at me. "It's not Dad."

"Really?"

"Really." She sounds like she's relieved too. She hands me the phone. Right now we're on the same team, Team Get Dad Home. Team Please Let It Work Out.

I walk upstairs to my room and shut the door. I know better than to talk in the bathroom, where everyone can hear what I'm saying. "Hey," I say, waiting to hear Frannie or Hazel on the other end.

"Rachel, hi. It's Tate."

I can't think. It feels like my brain is frozen inside my head. "Hi," I say. It's all I can manage to get out. I've never talked to Tate on the phone. I don't know why it feels big and important, because I talk to him at school all the time. But it does.

"Hi," he says. "I left my phone in my locker, so I looked up your number in the directory. That's okay, right? Sorry if I'm bothering you. You're not in the middle of eating dinner or anything, right?"

"No, not yet. And you're not bothering me." I try to talk slowly so I don't stumble over my words, but they fall out of my mouth before I can think them through. "We usually start eating pretty early, but we're waiting for my dad."

"Oh," he says. "Where is he?"

"Work," I say, leaning against my dresser.

"On Thanksgiving?"

"Yeah. He's on call, so he's at the hospital seeing patients." It sounds worse out loud. I wish I had kept it to myself. "What about you?"

"We're waiting for Adam to get back from hanging out with some of his high school friends. His phone is dead or off. My mom is freaking out. We were supposed to run together this morning in the Turkey Trot. We do it every year. I guess he forgot—" Tate stops himself. "That's why I called you, because you said, you know, you'd listen if I ever wanted to talk about Adam."

"I remember," I say. "I'm sorry he missed the race. I think I'd really hate it if a tradition got messed up, like if my dad didn't make it home to carve the turkey with me. That would be hard."

"Yeah. Exactly," he says. "I mean, it's okay, I guess."

"Not really," I say.

"The whole race I kept thinking maybe I messed up where we were supposed to meet and that he was mad at me."

"That's such a bad feeling."

"It stinks, because we didn't make the play-offs, so this was our only time to spend together until Christmas, you know?"

I nod. "Yeah. I really do." I listen for the garage. There's still nothing. I wonder if Mom has tried calling Dad yet. "I'm sorry about the play-offs."

"Thanks," he says.

"Are you going to say something?" I ask Tate. "To your brother."

"Yeah. He promised. He should have been there. Are you going to talk to your dad about working on Thanksgiving?"

"No." I shake my head. I'm not even sure I should be allowed to feel the way I do. "He's never going to change jobs or stop being on call. He's always going to work a lot. And with the new baby, he'll have even less time to spend with me. I'm pretty sure if I said something to him, I'd end up feeling worse."

"It might be hard. But you should," he says. "Even if it doesn't change how things actually are, I think it matters. Plus, you don't want to end up taking all your feelings out on your little bro."

"I'd never do that."

"You might. But you shouldn't. Little bros are the best. Trust me." I can tell he's smiling on the other end of the phone.

We're both quiet. I can hear him breathing, like a soft humming in my ear.

"I'm going to the formal," I say. "I wanted to tell you."

"Good," he says. "You were weird about it before."

"I know. Sorry about that. I thought I was going to have to wear my brace, but I don't have to now."

"It must be hard to worry about that," he says.

"Yeah," I say. "It's a big responsibility."

"I'm going too," he says.

"I know. You told me. Kyle is making you."

"Not anymore. I want to go now," he says. I smile. "Happy Thanksgiving, Rachel."

"Happy Thanksgiving," I say.

I walk downstairs and put the phone away. I sit down at the table next to Gram. Papa is dozing off in his chair—not because he's getting older, but because he likes to nap. He always has. "Who was that?" Gram whispers in my ear. "Boyfriend?"

I smile and shake my head, but I feel my cheeks burning. "I'm not sure if he wants to be my boyfriend. I mean, I think he does. I know he likes me."

"Did you know your mother had all kinds of admirers when she wore her brace?"

"That's not true," Mom says.

"It is true. And then after your surgery, all the boys in the neighborhood couldn't wait for you to come back to school. I think you were in your brace when Mike first asked you out."

"Who knows," Mom says. "Don't listen to her, Rachel. My brace was even bigger than yours. But maybe you're right about Mike."

"Of course I'm right," Gram says. "I still have that necklace he bought you."

I smile. Mom had a bigger brace than me and someone asked her out and bought her jewelry.

"Oh, and Gram sent me to school in a nightgown. Did I tell you that already? I'll never forgive you for that one, Ma." Mom shakes her head at Gram.

"It was a beautiful nightgown," Gram says.

"It was a *nightgown*!" Mom is almost shouting now.

"It didn't look like one. It had this gorgeous white lace." Gram stops talking and starts laughing. "Okay, now that I'm thinking about it. It looked a little like a nightgown."

"Thank you," Mom says.

"Mort, wake up," Gram says.

"I'm awake."

"No, you're not."

"How am I supposed to sleep when the two of you are still yelling about that nightgown twenty-five years later?"

Mom, Gram, and I all laugh.

"Did your mom tell you about the pencil?" Papa asks me.

I shake my head.

"She got itchy on her second or third day in the brace. So the genius sticks a pencil down the back of the thing when no one was home to help her, and it gets stuck."

"Do you have to tell her everything?" Mom says to Papa, like it's their secret.

"I want to know," I say.

"You do?" Mom asks, like that's the craziest thing she's ever heard.

"Yes," I say.

"She's part of it now," Papa says to Mom. "Family tradition!"

"I hadn't thought about it like that," Mom says.

Neither had I.

"Were you scared?" I ask Mom.

"No," she answers. "I was itchy."

We all laugh, and that's when the garage door rumbles. "He's here!" I cover my mouth with my hand, trying to catch the words before everyone can hear how desperate they sound.

"I hope you hadn't given up on me." Dad slams the door behind him. He has a stack of papers tucked between his arm and his suit jacket. "Morty, good to see you," he says, reaching out to shake Papa's hand. He kisses Gram on the cheek. "Please, don't get up." He puts his paperwork on the counter. "I'm sorry I'm late." Dad looks at Mom and then at me. I know he means it. He really is sorry.

"It's okay, honey," Mom says. "We're glad you're home. Everything is wonderful." And it's true. Dad is home, Tate likes me, and I'm in a club with Mom, Papa, and Gram.

"All right," Dad says, clapping his hands together. "Let's get to it." He looks at me and then walks over to the sink, so I know it's time to scrub up. Dad puts on the only apron I've ever seen in our house. It must have been Mom's at one point, because it has big, yellow ruffles, but Dad is the only one who wears it. I can't help but giggle as I wash my hands.

"No mocking allowed." He plugs in the electric knife, and it makes a loud rumbling sound. Mom, Gram, and Papa go into the other room so they can hear each other as they talk. Dad smiles at me and starts slicing.

I keep the counter clean and the empty serving trays coming, while he carefully carves and sorts the meat like a pro. "Was Mom mad?" he asks without taking his eyes off the buzzing knife.

"She's never mad," I say.

"Really?" he asks.

It's weird to me that Dad doesn't know the answer or that he needs to be reminded. I wait for him to ask about my feelings. I've already decided what I'm going to say: Not mad. Sad.

"What did your grandparents say about the brace?"

"Nothing, really." I wait for him to change the subject back, but he doesn't. I wish it wasn't like that. I want to be able to tell him things. I want him to know that I miss him and that sometimes I'm not sure how to talk to him. I have so much to say. Maybe I should just say it.

"I wasn't mad that you were late either, but it made me sad," I say. "I was scared you weren't going to make it home in time to do this."

He nods like he already knows that. “Me too,” he says, and it’s exactly what I needed to hear.

If I ever figure out how to be honest with Dad about everything, like Tate said I should, I’ll tell him that he isn’t bad at talking to me. He doesn’t need Mom. I’ll tell him about how she’s not so great at it lately. It’ll probably make him feel better to know he’s not the only one. That usually helps me. And I’ll ask him why he picked a job where he has to work so much. I don’t think it has to do with me specifically, but it would be nice to know for sure, so I wouldn’t have to wonder.

After dinner, I’m helping Mom clean up when I hear a bang. I dry off the plate I’m holding and follow the sound into the mudroom. Frannie is standing outside. Normally I wouldn’t be surprised to see her, since she lives only a few houses away, but it’s Thanksgiving, and her eyes are bloodshot and swollen. I open the door as fast as I can and wrap my arms around her as she comes inside. She falls further into me and starts to cry, or maybe she never stopped.

“Who’s there?” Mom asks from the kitchen. “Rachel? Is everything okay?” I feel Frannie pulling away. I hold on tighter.

Mom pokes her head in and sees what’s going on. “I’m sorry. I didn’t realize. Stay as long as you want, Frannie. We have plenty of food if you’re hungry. I’ll put a plate together for you, in case.” I listen to the charms on Mom’s bracelet fade away as she disappears into the kitchen.

"Can we go outside?" Frannie sounds like she's gasping for air.

"Let me get my coat." I run into the kitchen. "We're going outside to talk for a few minutes, okay?" I whisper to Mom.

"It's cold," she says. "Make sure you bundle up." I nod.

Frannie is leaning against the washing machine when I get back. She looks so small and brittle, about to crumble like a cracker. She's always so sure of herself, like she's coated in this hard, shiny shell, that it feels wrong seeing her broken down.

"Is your mom going to call my dad?" Frannie asks me on our way outside.

"No way." I have no idea what Mom is going to do, but it doesn't sound like Frannie will stay if she thinks her dad is coming over. It surprises me. They don't usually fight.

"Good. I'm not dealing with him right now."

I lead Frannie to my secret place under the deck. I've never taken anyone here before, but this is the kind of special occasion my hideout was built for. The lights from the kitchen and living room are on. Mom is about to serve tea and pie. The thought of hot chamomile with a drop of honey sends a chill down my legs, reminding me how cold it is out here.

Once we're under the deck, I turn on my mega flashlight so we can see each other. Frannie fades into the pink beanbag chair. I sit down on a pile of frozen mulch. I don't know if I'm supposed to ask what's going on. I look at my hands and wait for her to say something, but she doesn't start talking or crying. She's so quiet I'm afraid she might disappear.

"You know how you fight with your mom?" she says. "But it's because you're close, or because you're the same in all of these weird ways?"

I nod, even though I'm not sure if that's why I fight with my mom. Maybe it is. I don't know.

"My mom and I used to do that," she says. "But my dad doesn't fight. He's too sad. Or maybe he never liked to. I can't remember. Lucy is like him. I'm like my mom. I was. Now I'm like no one. I hate her for being dead. It's not fair."

I'm so sad for Frannie. I don't know what to say. I try to think about what I want or need when I'm sad, and then I do the only thing I can think of: I reach out and hold her hand. She lets me.

And I am thankful.

twenty-three

THE WEEK OF formal feels like it goes on forever. The only good part about not being a shoo-in for the A Team is that I'm so focused on prepping for tryouts and working out my right leg that I don't have as much time to obsess about the dance. Okay, I do have some time for that, but I have less time than I would if I wasn't practicing for soccer.

On Friday, my stomach is fluttering in anxious circles. I don't understand how teachers can expect us to sit through school today. I can't think about anything except for what it will be like if Tate asks me to dance or asks me out. It feels like everyone in the seventh grade is holding their breath all day, and when the last bell rings, it sounds longer and louder than usual.

Frannie stays at school to help finish decorating the winter wonderland. Hazel and I get ready at my house. I can tell Mom wants tonight to be special for me, because she orders the saucy, cheesy, delicious pizza from Sal's that I love. We eat and then curl our hair and paint our nails and toes to match our dresses. Hazel picks aquamarine, and I go with gold shimmer. Mom even lets us use her makeup, which is normally locked up and off-limits. Too bad she hardly has any good eye shadows. It's all boring browns and beiges. Hazel finds one that's sort of like eggplant, which is almost purple, and it looks good on both of us, especially with a lot of mascara.

After we're done with hair, nails, and makeup, I get to take off my brace. I don't have to put it back on until I get home from the formal! When Hazel goes into the bathroom to change into her outfit, I take the dress Mom and I bought out of the garment bag and step into it. The deep-gold fabric doesn't have sequins or glitter or anything like that, but it glistens when the light hits it the right way, and I feel like I'm sparkling. It has a sweetheart neckline, like the purple one Hazel and I both loved, and hugs my waist, then flares out into a small teacup shape. It's everything I imagined.

When Mom drops us off at school, she whispers, "Enjoy every minute. You look beautiful." It feels good to have her on my side tonight.

The gym has been transformed. There are swirls of cotton and white fabric with lace and crystal details everywhere I turn. The ceiling is covered with snowflakes, and tiny white lights are sprinkled around the room. Everything is shimmering, glittering, glistening. It's glowing with magic and hope. I love the way the light shines off my dress.

Hazel and I meet Frannie by the door like we planned. Her dress is winter white with a silver belt, and there are tiny crystals pinned into her waves. She matches the room.

Hazel squeals when she spots Kyle in his tie, which is color coordinated with her dress. Tate walks in next to him. I catch my breath. He looks that cute. He's wearing a blue blazer and a hunter green tie. I don't think I've ever seen him all dressed up before. Not like this. He smiles when he sees me, flashing a dimple, and his eyebrows go straight up, like something about me surprises him.

"Take a picture of us girls." Hazel points to the three of us and then hands Kyle her phone.

We all smile for the camera. I squeeze between Hazel and Frannie.

"Now you two get together." Hazel points at Tate and then me.

"Good luck with that, dude," Kyle says.

"Shut it. You know you're next," Hazel says back to him. We all laugh.

Tate walks over and puts his arm around me, resting his hand on my shoulder. "One, two, three, look happy," Hazel says. I don't even have to try.

Once Hazel and Kyle are finished with their photo shoot, we ditch the boys for the dance floor. The music is blasting.

I can feel the beat pumping through me. Without thinking, I start to tap along on my stomach, forgetting my brace drum isn't there. It's a weird feeling to miss something about the brace. I guess I thought that once it came off, I'd go right back to normal, but it doesn't seem like that exists anymore.

I keep looking over at the boys huddled on the other side of the room. I don't mean to stare at Tate, but it's hard not to look at him. He towers over everyone. Every time our eyes lock together, I'm afraid he's about to look away from me, so I force myself to break eye contact before he can.

After we've been dancing for a while, the boys move a few inches closer to the girls. Kyle comes over and starts dancing with Hazel. Ladan and the forwards pull Frannie away. I don't see Tate anywhere, and I don't feel like dancing alone or being Hazel and Kyle's third wheel, so I head toward the bathroom.

When I slip through the white curtain in the back of the gym, the hallway is empty except for Tate. "Hey," he says, taking a few steps closer.

"Hey." I sound out of breath. The tips of my fingers are tingling. The music inside the dance slows down to a soft, steady beat, and the DJ says something about finding a partner. I wonder if Tate notices.

"I need a break from being in there," he says. "Want to go outside?"

I nod and try not to look disappointed that he didn't ask me to dance. He turns around and opens the door that leads outside, holding it like he's waiting for me to go first.

His shoes drag against the cement as he follows me along the path. There are tiny spotlights in the grass shining up at us. I don't stop walking until we're in the dark, looking at the soccer field. He's so close I can feel his shoulder radiating against my bare arm. He smells like he always does. I close my eyes and try to inhale everything about this moment. "I bet you're cold," he says.

I am, but I don't want to say anything that might make this end. "It feels good out here," I say, but the wind picks up and my teeth start chattering.

Tate puts his arm around my shoulder and pulls me in. It's warm, and I fit perfectly. He's shaking a little too, and I wonder if he's nervous or cold or both. "You look pretty," he says. "I like your dress."

"Thanks," I say.

Out of nowhere, he leans into me and I feel his lips against mine. I can't believe this is happening. I'm kissing Tate. It's like nothing I've ever felt before. It's happy and warm and sweet. My stomach is fluttering so fast and my heart feels like it's trying to keep up. I hope he can't tell it's my first kiss. I keep waiting for him to stop and tell me I'm doing it wrong, but he doesn't. I try to follow his lips. Soft. Slow. Minty. Natural-ish.

I feel a clink, my front teeth knocking into his. *Err.*

Awkward. I'm pretty sure this is cold, hard proof that I'm the world's worst kisser. I shouldn't be allowed to make out with someone ever again. But Tate doesn't pull away from me. He keeps kissing me. Faster. Closer. Like he doesn't want it to end. I don't either. It's the best thing I've ever experienced. I want to stand here and keep kissing forever.

"Tate-O," Kyle calls from inside the gym. "Whatcha doing out here?"

"Sorry," Tate whispers softly in my ear. His nose is cold against my cheek. "Do you want to go back in?" He rubs my shoulders.

"Not really," I say. "It's cold, but I'd rather stay here. I like being with you."

"Me too," he says. "I mean, I like being with you too."

This time, I lean in and kiss him.

"Come out, come out, wherever you are," Kyle says.

We stop kissing. "We should probably go in," Tate says, but he doesn't move, and I can tell he doesn't want to go anywhere. He takes a long, deep breath. Then he turns around. I follow him back inside. My body is tingling. I can still feel his lips on mine.

Kyle is waiting for us. "Oh . . . Hi, Rachel." He draws my name out, dragging it through the air. I smile at him by accident. *Tate kissed me. He likes me.* The words sound weird even in my head, like they can't possibly be real. But they are. They really are.

"I hope I didn't interrupt anything," Kyle says in a way that makes it clear he means exactly the opposite of what he's saying. "What were you two doing out there?"

He's looking right at me like I'm the one who's supposed to answer, so I do. "It's none of your business," I say.

"Tate's my best friend, so actually it is my business," Kyle says. "Tell me. What were you doing?"

"Let it go," Tate says quickly.

"No can do," Kyle says.

"We like each other. Get over it." I look right at Kyle when I say it, because I know it's true. I mean, Tate kissed me. We just kissed. That means everything.

"Her?" Kyle points at me, but he's looking at Tate. "Seriously? You like *her*?"

I hold my breath and wait for Tate to say something. *Say yes. Say you like me.*

"I mean, dude, she's the Robo-Beast." I feel my heart beat faster and harder inside my chest. "But hey, if that's your thing, that's cool. I didn't realize you were into freaks."

"Stop," Tate says. "It's not like that." He's looking at the ground. "Nothing even happened."

I feel my heart collapse in my chest. *That's not true. How could he say that? Walk away, Rachel. Go.* Only I can't move. I'm frozen solid.

"Rachel, I love your dress." I look up as soon as I hear Ladan's voice. She must have just walked over. I really hope she didn't hear what happened, but by the way she's looking at me right now with sad sympathy eyes, I'm sure she did. "It's so pretty."

"Thanks." My words barely make it out, and before she can say anything else, I walk through the white curtain and back into the dance. I run over to Hazel, where it's safe.

"Where have you been?" She smiles at me. "Come dance."

I can't stop the tears from pouring out.

"What's wrong?"

I shake my head. I can't speak. I can't do anything but cry. She grabs my hand and pulls me out of the gym and into the main lobby. The lights are bright and blinding. I close my eyes and let her lead the way.

"Is everything okay, girls?" I hear one of the chaperones call after us.

"Everything's great," Hazel shouts back and grabs my wrist even tighter than before. When I hear the door shut behind us and the lock snap, I open my eyes. We're in the single stall bathroom by the cafeteria. My body looks limp and deflated in the mirror, like there's nothing left on the inside. Lines of black mascara streak across my face.

Hazel grabs a stack of paper towels and runs water over them for a few seconds. She places the warm towels on my cheeks and rubs away the makeup and tears.

I take a deep breath, but I can't stop crying.

"What's going on?" Hazel asks. "What happened?"

I don't even know where to start. "Tate kissed me," I say.

"Shut up! Kyle kissed me!" Hazel squeals. "Can you believe it? We had our first kiss on the same night. Wait, why are you crying? Did he not ask you out?"

"He's not going to," I say.

"He is. He likes you."

I shake my head.

"I know that for a fact," Hazel says. "Kyle told me."

"Did Kyle tell you he calls me the Robo-Beast?"

"No," she says. "No way. He would never say that."

"He just did."

"You probably heard him wrong," she says.

"I didn't." My voice comes out louder than I expect.

"You're pretty upset," she says.

"I wasn't upset then," I say.

"I really feel like you didn't hear him right. He knows you're my best friend. And he likes you. I swear. Let's go ask him."

"No," I shout, because that's the worst, most embarrassing idea ever.

"Come on," Hazel says. "Let's clear it up so we can have fun for the rest of the night. This bathroom is hot, and we're missing the best part of the dance."

"Go ahead," I say. "I don't want to do that. It'll make it worse."

"What do you want me to do?" she asks. "Should I break up with him because he called you Robo-whatever?"

"That's not what I'm saying."

"Then what are you saying?"

"Not that," I say.

"I'm sorry, but I really want to have fun tonight," Hazel says.

"So go. I'm not trying to stop you," I say.

"I defend you a lot." Hazel raises her voice. "Like all the time in practice, and other times too."

"What are you talking about? The soccer girls like me."

"Not all the time. I mean, everyone makes fun of you. Even Frannie. You don't know the half of it. It's not just Kyle. I mean, he's the only one who'd say it to your face. And I'm sick of it. Every time something good happens to me, I have to worry about you and your brace and how it will make you feel. I'm sorry, but I don't feel like it tonight. I feel like having fun, because it's my seventh grade formal too. I want to dance with my boyfriend and be excited that I just had my first kiss ever. And for once I'm not going to let you ruin it."

Before I can say anything else, Hazel walks out and slams the door behind her.

I'm alone. I'm a puddle on the floor of the bathroom. I take my phone out of my bag and call home.

"Hello?" Mom answers.

I start crying as soon as I hear her voice.

"I'm coming," she says. "I'm coming right now."

twenty-four

MOM DOESN'T ASK questions on the ride home, and I don't turn on my music, so it's quiet in the car. After she pulls into the garage, she takes my hand in hers and says, "If you want to talk about anything, I'm here to listen, and I am sorry about whatever happened tonight that made you so upset."

I want to tell her, but I can't. Not now.

I put my brace back on and get into bed. I'm ready for this night to be over. I wish I had a playlist about heartbreak and hurt feelings ready right now to match my mood, but I don't. I always use music to pick myself up. I've never wanted to wade around in my own sadness until now.

My phone buzzes. It's Frannie: You okay? Hazel told me what happened. Seriously, don't sweat it. You guys will make up. And no one is even talking about the Robo-Beast thing anymore. None of it is a big deal. I swear.

It's a big deal to me, I write back.

It shouldn't be, she says. Really.

I don't want to talk about it. I'm shutting my phone off. I don't want to hear all the reasons why I shouldn't let it bother me. I can't help how much it hurts that everyone makes fun of my brace behind my back, even Frannie.

I don't turn my phone back on for the rest of the weekend. I don't take any time out of the brace either, except to shower, making up the hours I missed so I could go to the stupid, stupid dance. I spend most of my time listening to sad music with a beat, so I can still drum along, and practicing for tryouts. I stay focused on developing my right leg. I know that if I can get to the point where kicking and passing on that side feels natural, I'll make the A Team. And I still want to, more than anything.

On Sunday night, Mom and I watch an Agatha Christie series on PBS and dip homemade chocolate brownies with mint chips into hot chocolate. I try not to think about what Hazel and Tate and Kyle said and didn't say, because when I do, I can't breathe. I thought that by the time the end of the weekend finally rolled around I'd feel better and be ready to face my real life. I was wrong.

"Can I stay home tomorrow?" I ask Mom. "Please?"

"Are you sick?" She rests her hand on my forehead.

I shake my head. "But I don't feel well," I say softly. "Can that count?"

"You can take the day off if you want, but if you don't go to school, you won't be able to try out for soccer."

"Oh. Yeah. I forgot about that rule," I say. "Never mind."

"You might feel better if you talk about what happened."

I shrug. "Tate and I kissed," I say before I can think about it for too long and stop the words from coming out of my mouth.

"Ooh." Mom's voice goes all the way up, like she's surprised. Then she takes a deep breath and asks, "So . . . how was it?"

"The kissing part was good, but then . . ." I shake my head. "One of his friends—Kyle. He figured out what happened and started saying all these mean things about me. Then Tate denied that we kissed. And when I told Hazel everything, she said there was no way that Kyle actually called me a Robo-Beast, even though he did." Mom claps her hands over her mouth. "But then Hazel said it wasn't just Kyle. Everyone talks about how my brace is weird, even Frannie. And Frannie said it wasn't that bad and I shouldn't be upset."

"Rachel. Honey." Mom looks right at me. There are tears in her eyes. "It is that bad." She wraps her arms around me and pulls me into her, rocking me back and forth and holding on as tight as she can, like she's trying to protect me. "I'm so sorry."

We stay like that for a few minutes.

"Want to hear the good news?" Mom asks.

I shrug, because there is no good news.

"It can't get any worse," she says.

"Umm, how is *that* good news?" I ask.

"Everything bad happened already, and it couldn't have been worse, but you survived it. You're on the other side." She takes another deep breath and puts her hands to her heart. "And what makes me so proud is that you didn't let any of the horrible things that anyone said stop you from practicing for tryouts and doing everything you can to get what you want. That takes a lot of strength. More than you probably realize."

I nod, because I hadn't thought about myself that way—as strong—until now.

"So the good news is that from this moment, it's only going to be easier."

I smile, because in a weird way that does feel like good news.

Before bed, I make a new playlist. It's a mix of anthems and fight songs that remind me there's nowhere to go but up.

On Monday, Mom drops me off a little later than usual, so I don't have to talk to anyone before school starts. That was her idea. She thought it would help me ease back into things. But as soon as I get out of the car, I see Frannie standing outside. There's no way to avoid her. I turn around to get back in the car, but Mom is gone. I don't remember hearing her drive away.

Frannie runs her fingers around the ends of her blonde

ringlets. She must have slept in thick curlers, because her waves are the big, bouncy kind. My hair is still wet.

"Where have you been?" Frannie says as soon as I get close enough. "We were supposed to get ready for tryouts together. I called and texted you all weekend."

"I shut my phone off. I told you I didn't want to talk."

"Hazel is so upset. I decided we're all going to talk about what happened at lunch."

"I don't want to talk to Hazel," I say. "And we're not having lunch."

"You have to at least give her a chance to explain," Frannie says.

"No, I don't." I grab the door handle.

"Rachel, hold on." Frannie puts her hand on mine.

I push it away. I want her to know I'm serious.

"Kyle is such an idiot," she says, like he's the only reason I'm upset. "It's not like anyone else actually thinks that stuff about you. I mean, Hazel and I don't."

"I bet you don't," I say. "But you don't know what Hazel really thinks."

"Yes, I do."

"You weren't there. You didn't hear what she said."

Frannie rolls her eyes. "I can't believe you're turning this into something it's not. What happened is not a big deal."

"Everyone talking about me behind my back feels like a big deal—"

"It's just Kyle."

"I'd be over it by now if it were just Kyle." I hate that she's lying to me. "Hazel said that you make fun of me."

"That's not true. He's the only one. Who cares what he says? No one."

"Then why don't you tell him about your mom? You don't know what it feels like. No one can see what's wrong with you."

I feel terrible as soon as the words come out of my mouth.

Frannie looks stunned. She winces, then opens the door and walks inside.

I didn't mean it, but it's too late to take it back now. I wait a few minutes to give her time to get away from me. Then I walk into school. The heat is blasting, but I leave my coat on. I'm going to sweat it out, because the extra wool-cashmere-cotton layers make me feel stronger. And right now I'd do just about anything to feel something other than alone and awful.

The hallway is empty and quiet, except for the radiators humming and clanking. Every classroom door is closed. I'm late, and I have science first period.

I close the door to the lab behind me and keep my head down, trying not to draw extra attention to myself. I can feel everyone's eyes on me, following me across the room. "Nice of you to join us, Ms. Brooks," Mr. Hsu says.

"I'm sorry," I mumble without looking up.

"Let's get to it." Mr. Hsu claps his hands. "Rachel, Tate can fill you in on what we'll be doing today."

My stomach aches when he says Rachel and Tate back-to-back, like our names belong together, when they don't. Not anymore. Not ever. I'm so mad at Tate. I hate him for making me think he actually wanted to be my boyfriend. Here's what I realized over the weekend: Tate likes me and wants to kiss me, but he doesn't want to admit either of those things or stand up for me in front of Kyle.

When I get to our table, I put my bag on the chair instead of on the ground, so I don't have to bend over to pull out my notebook and pen. I pick up the instructions for the lab, walk to the other side of the room, and collect the materials listed on the paper. I know Tate is trailing me, but I don't care or want his help. I carry everything over to our table and start reading the instructions out loud. "Pour vinegar into the bottle until—"

"Rachel." He stops me.

I look right at him for the first time since he kissed me. I wish he didn't look so cute and that his eyes didn't sparkle and that he would stop looking at me like he actually cares what I have to say, when he doesn't. Everything Tate has ever done makes me feel pathetic. I want him to fix what happened at the dance. I want him to say he's sorry and go tell Kyle how much he likes me and make it better now. I don't want our kiss to mean nothing, when it mattered to me.

"You forgot your goggles," he says, picking them up off the table and holding them out for me.

"That's why you stopped me?" My voice comes out too loud.

"Safety first." He grins.

I don't smile back or say anything, because it's not funny. I take the goggles, cover my eyes, and start reading the instructions again.

For the rest of class, I keep waiting for him to apologize, but he doesn't mention the dance or the kiss or anything other than science, like he thinks I'm just going to forget what he did to me. And the only good part about the way he's acting is that it makes me like him less.

Thankfully Hazel isn't in any of my classes, except for gym, and I don't go to gym anymore. I manage to avoid her all morning. At lunch, I carry my food over to an empty table in the back corner. I don't look over at Hazel when I hear her laughing, or when I hear her say "Rachel." A few minutes later, she sits down next to me.

"I'm sorry," she says.

I take a bite of my sandwich.

"Frannie told me not to bother you. She said you would talk to us when you were ready, but I wanted to say it in person. I'm really sorry."

I glance over at her. Her eyes are glossy, like she's about to cry or she's been crying. I know she's sorry. She's sorry we had a fight and that I'm hurt and probably that I'm going through this, because before I got the brace, we never had an argument, not one. I want to forgive her for everything and have the whole thing be over, because this is a million times worse for me than it is for her. She's the one with the boyfriend and the matching formal outfits who is almost definitely going to make the A Team. I'm the Robo-Beast.

But I'm mad that she won't flat out admit what Kyle said about me, and I guess I'm a little mad that he's still her boyfriend after how he treated me. The part that hurts the most is that she didn't have my back when the worst thing that has ever happened to me happened. "I needed you," I say. "And you left me."

"I know." She takes a deep breath.

"That's not going away for a while."

Hazel nods. Then she stands up and walks away.

After school, I head to the locker room and change for tryouts. I'm not talking to Hazel or Frannie, which means I have no one to stand next to during warm-ups or partner off with for passing. I have to walk over to Coach Howard and ask to be paired with someone. "Does anyone else not have a partner?" Coach Howard announces.

A hand goes up in the back. It's a nervous-looking sixth grader who didn't play in the regular soccer season.

"Okay, great. Now you do," she says. "Rachel, grab a ball and head on over there." I can hear people laughing. I don't turn around to see who it is. I need to block it out and concentrate on playing my best. I want to make the A Team. I'm going to.

It turns out Jenna, my new passing partner, has never played soccer before, but she does pretty well for her first time. I even help her work on following through, which is fun, especially when she gets better.

After that, Coach Howard has us run drills, every kind imaginable: kicking and shooting and agility. I stay focused, even when I have to guard Hazel. I keep my eyes on the ball and pretend she's someone else, someone who didn't used to be my best friend.

I control the ball, and without thinking, I use my right foot to clear it, as if kicking with my right leg is instinctive, even though it's not. It's practice. All the hard work—dribbling and shooting and strengthening my right side—is finally starting to pay off and make a difference.

Coach Howard watches every player closely and scribbles a lot of things on her clipboard. I hope she's writing that I'm on the A Team.

twenty-five

I'M SITTING ON my bed after school, wrapped in a fluffy ball of blankets, reviewing my science notes and jamming out on my brace drums to "We Are the Champions." I'm at the part about "fighting 'til the end" when I feel the pages spread out in front of me vibrate. I pat around for my phone. Do you think we need to memorize the periodic table? It's Tate.

I stare at his message. I don't get why he's sending me a stupid text about science. I'm not writing back and pretending everything is fine. He needs to apologize to me and leave me alone or apologize and ask me out. Those are his only options.

Someone knocks at the door. I know it's Mom before she even opens it, because Dad is on call at the hospital, and he wouldn't come up here even if he were home. He's afraid of all the cranberry- and cream-colored ruffles.

“Come in,” I say when Mom knocks a second time.

I check my phone to see if Tate has said anything else. Nope.

“I came to see what you’re doing up here.” Mom says it like it’s weird for me to study in my room.

“I have a big science test on Friday.” I glance down at my notes.

“I can see that.” She sits down next to me and runs her fingers through my dry, tangled hair, tucking a few pieces behind my ear. It feels good. Really good. “Can I bring you anything?”

I shake my head.

Mom smiles. Without makeup to brighten her eyes, I can see how tired they are. I bet she misses Dad. I know I do. I’m glad she’s here, checking on me. It makes me feel less alone.

“We’re going to see Dr. Paul tomorrow,” she says, “to make sure your brace is working.”

My chest tightens. “No. I can’t.”

“I spoke to the principal’s assistant a few hours ago. Someone from each of your classes is going to collect your homework, and we can pick it up on our way back from Boston. They promised you wouldn’t be penalized in any way.”

“No,” I say. It stings behind my eyes. *No. No. No.* “I have tryouts tomorrow. If I don’t show up, I won’t even have a chance at making the A Team.”

“We’ll try our best to get you there in time.”

“That’s not good enough. Coach Howard is going to think

I knew about this appointment, even though I didn't. Even though nobody told me."

"This is not a negotiation. We're going. It's important." Mom stands up and walks over to the door, so I know the conversation is over. "You don't have a choice."

"I never do," I say.

She sighs. "Is there something else I can do to make it better? Other than cancel?"

I try to think of something that could make this easier for me. "Can Dad come with us?" I look up at her.

"You know how busy he is, honey."

"If this appointment is really important, he should be there. I want him there."

She nods. "I'll try to make it work for next time."

"Just reschedule. Please." My voice sounds strained. "Then I won't have to miss tryouts and Dad can come with us."

"Do you think I like dragging you to the doctor? Do you think this is fun for me?" Her voice is loud and strained, like she's trying not to scream at me. "This is exactly why I don't tell you about the appointments ahead of time. You act like a baby."

"I hate Dr. Paul!"

"No, you don't." She brushes my words away.

"Yes, I do." I'm not backing down.

She walks back over and stands next to my bed. "He's an old-school surgeon," she says, like that's a totally reasonable excuse for how he acts.

"He never talks to me, Mom. He doesn't explain anything. He acts like I'm not even in the room until it's time to examine me! And that's even worse."

"You don't have to tell me that. I went through so much more. You can't even imagine."

"Then why are acting like you don't get it?" I ask.

"You've blown these appointments up in your head. You've turned them into something they're not. It's ten minutes in the room with him, if that, and then it's over. You don't need to act like the world is crashing down around you, Rachel."

"I'm naked, Mom," I shout. "I'm standing there naked and they're all staring at me and pointing and talking about me and quizzing each other in medical code about my problems like I'm not in the room. I have no idea how long we're in there, because I'm so uncomfortable and it feels like it's never going to end. I hate all those eyes on me. And then you treat me like there's something wrong with me that I don't feel lucky to be there. I can't go back. I'm not doing it." There are tears pouring down my cheeks. I don't bother to wipe them away. "Please don't make me. Please."

She looks at me and covers her mouth. Her eyes fill up with tears. She's seeing my appointments the way I see them for the first time. She sits down next to me on my bed, sinking into the mattress. "I didn't know." Her words sound broken, falling out of her mouth.

"What do you mean you didn't know? I don't understand.

You went through the same thing. I don't get why you're acting like you have no idea what it's like for me."

"I can't remember any of the things you just described," she says. "I mean, I know a lot of those same things happened to me, but the feelings aren't there. It's more like facts that I memorized—cold hands and long white coats." She swallows hard. "I had no idea how it felt for you. I'm so sorry, Rachel."

"I thought I didn't have to explain it to you, because you understood."

She nods. "I thought that too."

"Why don't you remember?" I ask.

She sighs. "My first surgery was such a long time ago. Gram, Papa, and I—we never talked about it. I think it was too painful and scary for all of us. We were just trying to get through it." That must be why Papa was crying at Thanksgiving. "Then after my recovery was over, we wanted to move forward and pretend the brace and the fusion never happened. I think I'm really starting to deal with everything that I went through for the first time now, twenty-five years too late. I guess it's harder for me than I even realize. Do you understand what I'm saying?"

I nod, because I think I do. It explains a lot about why Mom is the way she is. "I didn't know you had more than one surgery," I say.

"I had one when I was your age, and another about two years after you were born. I was having a lot of pain from the rods and screws in my back, and by that point, my fusion had healed and I didn't need them anymore. Eventually my pain got so bad that they had to be removed. Dr. Paul did the second surgery. I was so afraid. They were trying to put me to sleep, and I was crying. I couldn't stop, so he came into the operating room and sat with me. He rubbed my head until I fell asleep. No doctor had ever done that for me before. I'd never felt so safe. I guess I assumed you'd feel the same way with him."

"I didn't know that," I say.

"Does it matter?"

"I don't know." I don't want it to. It's weird to think of Dr. Paul as someone who took care of Mom. "I still don't want to go."

"I wish you didn't have to," she says. "But you do, which means we need to come up with a plan so it's more comfortable for you to be there. I want you to feel safe."

I think about it for a moment. "It would really help if you could find a way to ditch the extra doctors."

"I'll try my best to make that happen for you."

I nod. "Can you do something so that my gown doesn't fall off?"

"I can definitely do that."

"Thank you," I say. "You're going to ask Dad to come, right? And also check to see if there's a way for me to get to tryouts on time? Because I really want to be there."

"I'll do everything I can," she says. "I promise."

~

TO: Coach Howard
SUBJECT: Tomorrow

Hi Coach Howard,
I just found out that I have a doctor's appointment tomorrow for my back, and even though it starts in the morning, they always go really, really late, because we have to wait forever! So there's pretty much no chance I'm going to be at tryouts tomorrow, unless there's some kind of miracle. Also, I'm sorry for not telling you earlier. I would have, but I just found out. I promise I'm going to do everything I can to get there.

Also, I wanted to tell you, in case you didn't already know, that I really, really, really (x one million) want to make the A Team. If there's anything I can do to make up for missing tryouts tomorrow, I will. I hope you get this email before tryouts start, and that there is something I can do.

Thank you,
Rachel (Brooks)

twenty-six

WHEN I GET downstairs the next morning, Dad is sitting at the kitchen table in a suit drinking a cup of coffee. The newspaper is unfolded in front of him, but he isn't reading it. He's talking to Mom about one of the headlines. He keeps saying the name of some politician who I only sort of recognize. Neither of them notices me.

It's Tuesday. I'm pretty sure Dad should have left for work hours ago. The only other time I can remember him being home on a weekday was before Grandma's funeral.

"Who died?" I ask.

Mom and Dad both stop everything. Dad looks at Mom, like he's waiting for her to speak on their behalf. He isn't sure how to talk to me without her help.

"No one," she says. "Stop being so dramatic. Dad is coming to the doctor with us." Mom is acting as if everything is totally normal and we didn't fight last night. We're the kind of family where everything is fine in the morning even if it's not.

"Oh." I try not to sound too surprised, but I don't get it. Dad always has to work, but today, on a random Tuesday, when we're doing *this*, he's free. "Why?" I ask.

"Don't sound so excited." I can't tell if Dad is offended or kidding or something else entirely.

"I'm sorry," I say. "I'm confused."

"You don't have to be sorry," Dad says to me.

"Yes, she does," Mom says to Dad, but she's looking at me. I wonder if Mom asked Dad to come because of what I said last night and he actually made it happen.

"Amy," he says. "Rachel has probably never seen me at home on a weekday morning before."

Mom doesn't say anything else. We both know that Dad is the only one who can talk about the fact that he's never around.

"Come over here." He waves his paper at me. "Sit down and eat something before we have to get going. I cooked." He points to the two cereal boxes on the table and puts a bowl in front of me. "I'm going with you because I'm your father and I want to be there." He pours me a bowl of cereals mixed together. "I know how badly you want to make it to tryouts. We're going to do everything we can to get you there, okay?"

I nod. "Why haven't you ever come with us before?" I ask.

"Work," he says. "You know that."

"Why do you have to work so much?"

He shakes his head like he's surprised by my question. "Why do you ask?"

"I just want to know," I say.

Dad crosses his arms and looks around the room, then back at me. "I'm trying my best to take care of everyone who needs me."

I nod. "So why don't you have to work today?"

"Mom told me you really wanted me to be here. She said you told her it was important to you. I took that seriously."

"Thank you," I say and hug him. "I'm glad you're coming with us."

"Me too," he says.

Dad walks up to the desk in the hospital and checks us in while Mom and I stake out three seats in the far corner of the waiting room. We're usually in the main waiting area for an hour, sometimes two, before we're told to go anywhere, so we always bring plenty to do. Mom takes out the blue cotton yarn and knitting pattern she was working on in the car, and I open my science notes and put in my headphones. I'm doing this new thing where I only listen to one playlist on repeat. I don't feel like mixing it up. I guess I want something to feel the same. I try to zone out, except the only thing I can think about from the minute I sit down is getting out of here in time to make tryouts.

Dad sits down next to Mom and yawns loudly. It sounds like a lion roaring.

"Rachel Brooks," a nurse calls out over the speaker. She looks down at my chart and says, "Please head to x-ray."

"Is something wrong?" I ask.

Dad laughs. Mom rolls her eyes like she knows something I'm supposed to know too.

"I don't get it," I say. "What did I miss?"

"Get used to it," she says, packing up her knitting. "Your dad is here. Everything is going to go much faster today."

I cross my fingers. I really hope she's right about that.

We follow the signs for the x-ray department down an endless white corridor. I want to sprint down the hall, but Mom can't move very fast these days. The baby really slows her down. We finally get in the elevator, and I hold my breath as the red numbers flash above us. I hope no one with a hospital badge recognizes either of my parents. I'm never in the mood to smile and pretend I care about someone who hasn't seen me since I was "this big," but especially not today.

Dad walks up to the counter and says something to one of the x-ray techs. She looks at her screen and then at me. "Come right this way," she says, as if Dad has some magical power that lets us skip to the front of every line.

After they're finished taking my x-rays, I change back into my clothes, all of them, even though I'm not supposed to. I don't want to walk down the halls or sit in the waiting room in just a gown. I walk as fast as I can down the long hallway toward the waiting area. "You're supposed to keep your gown on," the x-ray tech shouts from behind me.

I don't stop or turn around. I say, "Thank you," and keep walking.

"Please put your gown back on." Her sneakers squeak against the floor.

I push through the doors and walk into the waiting room before she can catch me. It's the first time I've ever broken one of the hospital rules. I keep waiting for her to grab my shoulder and drag me back in there. But she doesn't. Nothing happens.

I look around for my parents. Nearly all of the seats are full now with rows of people waiting to be x-rayed. After I sit down next to Mom and Dad, I check my phone. No emails. No texts. No missed calls. No reply from Coach Howard.

We only wait an hour before my name is called again, and we're back in the little white examining room, waiting to see the doctor.

The door opens and Dr. Paul walks in, followed by his flock of residents, flooding in behind him like pigeons. They fill every inch of extra space, sucking up the oxygen.

Dr. Paul's face lights up when he sees Dad sitting between Mom and me. I've never seen him smile before. "David, it's been too long," he says.

Dad stands up and shakes his hand.

"I haven't seen you since . . . well, since you were standing here." He points to the residents. That's when I realize that Dr. Paul was Dad's teacher.

"Thank you for everything you've done for Rachel." Dad sounds sincere.

I bite my tongue hard. I've never seen Dad look at anyone the way he's gazing at Dr. Paul. He's wide-eyed. Dad is always the most important doctor in the room—at least, any room I've ever been in—and right now there's someone whose opinion matters more. It's weird.

Dr. Paul pulls up two x-rays on the computer monitor and measures the curve in my spine on both, the one from my last appointment and the one from today. The room is silent. I watch the clock and try to ignore Dr. Paul's loafer *tap, tap, tapping* against the floor. I'm getting worried that something is wrong, because it's been almost five minutes since anyone said a word.

Dr. Paul takes a deep breath. "From the x-ray, it appears that the curve has moved to thirty-three degrees."

I look at Dad. His face has the same composed look it usually does. Mom's head is hanging in front of her, limp and wilted like a half-dead flower.

"It's worse than before," Dr. Paul translates.

No. No. No. I don't want to have surgery. I never should have gone to the stupid dance. I didn't mean to make it worse.

"Amy, I assume Rachel has been compliant." He looks at Mom.

She lifts her head up. "Rachel has been the perfect patient. I don't understand how this is happening. She's done everything right."

"Mom, I haven't." The words spill out of my mouth before I can stop them.

"Yes. You have." Mom's voice comes out sharp and defensive.

I shake my head. "One time I took an extra long shower after practice so I could have a few more minutes out of the brace. And the dance . . . I'm so sorry."

"Rachel. Honey." She rubs my shoulder. "It's okay. That's a very small amount of time. It wouldn't have made a difference."

"You're right, Amy," Dr. Paul says to Mom. "But this time is very critical, so between now and when she's done growing, let's aim for perfection. We want to make sure Rachel does everything she can to avoid having her curve progress."

I can still feel Mom's hand on my shoulder. She's ready to protect me.

Dr. Paul looks at my chart and then up at his students. "There are two indicators that the patient will be done growing soon. She hasn't grown since she was here for her last visit about four months ago. And she's had her period for two years."

I look at the ground and then at the ceiling and try to pretend no one is talking about my period right now.

"Rachel, why don't you come on up here so we can have a look at your back?"

Everyone looks at me. I can't believe I have to do this with Dad in the room.

"Excuse me." Dad looks down at his phone. It's been silent all day. "I need to follow up with a few patients."

Dad leaves and Mom stands up. She walks over and whispers something in Dr. Paul's ear. He thinks about whatever she said for a few seconds, then says something to the resident standing next to him, and they all file out, like it was that easy the whole time.

Mom sits down, and even though her mouth is closed, she's smiling. I know they're gone for good.

"Thank you," I whisper in her ear.

Mom rests her hand on the back of my neck and pulls me close to her. "I love you," she says.

"How's school?" Dr. Paul asks me. I have a feeling that Mom asked him to talk directly to me. It makes me extra glad I told her everything.

"Not great," I say.

"Rachel," Mom says.

"What? I'm telling the truth." I look at her. She doesn't say anything, but she lets go of my hand. She doesn't take her eyes off me.

I look at the clock. 2:30 p.m. One hour until tryouts start. "I'm probably going to miss my huge, really important soccer tryouts," I say to Dr. Paul. "And if I were there, if I got my chance to play, I'd probably make the A Team."

"I understand," he says. "Why don't I write you a note explaining that this appointment was very important?"

I think about his offer for a minute. It probably can't hurt to have a doctor's note, especially if I get to tryouts late. I might need something extra to convince Coach Howard I really do deserve a shot. "That might help," I say.

"Good," Dr. Paul says. "That's all I'm trying to do."

Mom clears her throat and stares at me like I'm forgetting something.

"Thank you very much for writing the note." I try to be very specific, because I'm only thankful for that part.

"You're welcome," he says. "Now, if you could change back into your gown, I'll do my best to get you out of here as quickly as possible."

After I change, I stand in front of Dr. Paul like usual. He takes out the measuring device, and Mom stands up. She walks over to me and grabs both sides of my gown. When I bend forward, it doesn't fall at all. For the most part, everything that should stay covered does. Dr. Paul runs the Scoliometer over my back and *hmms* like always.

"All right," he says at last. "You're all set."

I stand up. "Is thirty-three bad?" I ask, because in my head it sounds a lot bigger than thirty.

Dr. Paul looks surprised. "It's a good thing you've been

wearing the brace. It's working hard to keep your curve from moving. I don't think you'll be growing anymore. That's what I was explaining earlier. I'm hoping that when you come back in about two months, you'll be finished."

"With the brace?" I ask.

"Based on when you got your first period and the fact that you haven't grown since our last appointment, yes. We'll take an x-ray of your wrist at your next visit."

"Why would you take an x-ray of my wrist?" I ask. Since I've actually gotten Dr. Paul to talk to me for once, I'm going to keep it going and get all the answers.

"It'll show the growth plates of the individual bones in your hand. As you reach skeletal maturity, these bones start to close, and they have a pattern of closure that we've found to be reliable in determining if you're done growing."

"Wait. Hold up," I say. "You're telling me that the next time I'm here, I could be done with the brace."

He nods.

OMG! OMG! OMG! YES! Best day ever! Two months is not even that long. I can totally handle two months. It will still be indoor soccer season, and the baby won't be able to walk or talk or even hold his head up. There are fireworks going off inside of me, and the air tastes sweet and sugary, like blue cotton candy, every time I breathe.

I look at the clock. 2:45 p.m. Tryouts start in forty-five minutes. It will be tight, but I might actually make it.

~

Dad is waiting by the elevators. "Let's go." He waves us over.

"Wait," Mom says. "Don't we have to—" She points to the main desk.

"I took care of it." Dad hands each of us a business card with the date and time of my next appointment, aka the day I'm getting my brace off! Tuesday, February 10 at 10 a.m.

I think about texting Hazel and Frannie my news. I wish I wasn't in a fight with my best friends so they could be excited for me too.

In the car, I make a list of things I can't do right now that I will be able to do on Tuesday, February 10:

1. Play soccer without my brace.
2. Wear just a white cotton shirt.
3. Not feel itchy.
4. Forget to count time.
5. Eat an entire box of macaroni and cheese.

We get stuck in traffic on the way out of the city, and I spend the rest of the ride to school switching between watching the road and watching the clock. We pull into the visitors' parking lot at 3:30 p.m. exactly, which means tryouts are starting right now.

I grab my bag and run as fast as I can toward the gym. Dad

is running right behind me. It's dismissal time, so everyone is standing outside waiting for buses or parents to take them home. I don't stop until we make it to the gym.

Everyone is already dressed and starting to stretch. I walk right up to Coach Howard, and Dad follows me. "Rachel," Coach says, like she's surprised to see me.

"I made it!" I say, catching my breath.

"Well, what are you waiting for? Go change," she says, smiling.

"Thank you!"

Coach shakes her head. "Thank yourself. It was very responsible of you to let me know about your appointment as soon as you found out. It shows me you're dedicated to soccer and capable of handling your commitments."

"I'm really, really dedicated to soccer!" I say. Then I turn around and grin at Dad.

"A Team, here you come," he says.

~

Once we're done warming up, Coach Howard has us run two-on-three drills. I start on defense.

Frannie and I both sprint out from the goal line. She runs to cover Hazel, who has the ball, and I rush to cover the area between Ladan and Josie. Hazel passes the ball to Ladan. Ladan dribbles forward, and I can tell she is going for the goal, because she's setting up to shoot with her right foot, which is the only one she ever uses. I put my right leg up and block the shot with my shin. I get control of the ball. Ladan sprints over to me and tries to get the ball back, but I dribble away from her, bend forward, and box her out with my brace. Then I ping the ball to Frannie and she clears it.

"Where did that come from?" Ladan says under her breath.

I smile.

We switch positions, and I get a chance on offense. I'm in the middle, Frannie is on my right, and Josie is on my left with the ball. If Frannie and I weren't in a fight, this would be perfect. She'd try extra hard to make me look good. Still, I can do this. I know I can. I just need to use my right foot. *Focus.*

Coach Howard blows the whistle and Hazel runs to cover Josie, so tightly that Josie can hardly move. She doesn't have a choice but to pass the ball to me.

I tap the ball to Frannie and then run between the two defenders just in time for her to slide the ball back to me. I aim for the corner of the net with my right foot. Shoot, and follow through. The ball goes into the goal. *YES!*

Josie looks at me like she just bit into a lemon.

Frannie puts her hand in the air. I slap it and grin. We both jog to the back of the line. "That rocked," she says to me. "I can't believe how much stronger you're getting on your right side."

"I know, right?" I smile at her. "Thank you, brace."

"Seriously," she says. "I hope you know you're crushing tryouts."

"I do." I nod. I want to keep talking, to tell her I miss her and I'm sorry for what I said, but before I have a chance, Coach Howard blows the whistle and says, "Huddle up." And we both jog over to the rest of the team.

At the end of day two, I know deep down in my gut that I gave it my all. I hope my all is enough to make the A Team.

When I get home from soccer, I'm bored. I already finished my homework, because I've been going to the library during every free period. For the record, I'd definitely rather have best friends and have to do my homework after school than get everything done early and be able to do whatever I want by myself. I'm playing around on my phone when I decide to search "scoliosis," "back braces," and "friends," because I can't stop thinking about any of those things.

I don't know what I'm looking for exactly, but one of the first things that comes up is a video called "Top 10 Reasons to Love Your Back Brace." It was made by a girl named Mia, except, she says, that's not her real name, because her mom didn't want her to put her actual name online. She's in seventh grade too and she's really serious about basketball. I have this feeling we'd be friends if she lived outside Boston instead of Chicago. She says she's had her brace since fifth grade! And it's going to be at least two more years before she gets it off, because she only got her period a few months ago. I can't believe she's talking about her period online, but I think it's cool that she's so open about everything. I want to be more like that. She only has to wear her brace for twenty hours a day, which is better than twenty-three, but still, four years is a long time.

Here are the "Top 10 Reasons to Love Your Back Brace" (by Mia):

1. You can name it. I named mine Beatrice the Brace.
2. You can use your brace to get out of things you don't want to do. Examples to try: cleaning, carrying heavy boxes, carrying anything, and gym class.
3. It helps with your posture.
4. It keeps you warmer in the winter.
5. No one can tickle you on your sides. And it's kind of funny when people try, because when they hit something hard, they look confused and then you get to laugh at them!
6. You have your own personal musical instrument wherever you go. So start drumming.
7. You can stick pushpins in your brace and freak people out. It's really funny!
8. You can draw on your brace and have people sign it and make it look cool, because it's all yours! (P.S. Use rubbing alcohol to clean off

the designs if you mess up or want to start all over again.)

9. You can join the Curvy Girls and make new friends who also have back braces and are going through a lot of the same things.
10. Because dealing with it is hard, it makes you realize you can handle pretty much anything that comes your way.

I love all of Mia's ideas, especially the ones I never would have thought of in a million years. I search for "Curvy Girls scoliosis" online and find out it's a network of these peer support groups for kids with scoliosis. I don't think it makes sense to join now, since I probably have only two months left in my brace, but it's nice to know it's there, in case I change my mind. Also, I love that Mia mentions drumming on her brace, because it's my favorite thing. Mostly it helps to hear someone else talk about the good parts of having a brace, like somehow all of those things, even the ones I've already thought of, feel more true and real when Mia says them.

twenty-seven

THE NEXT DAY in science, I'm standing at one end of the table setting up the lab, and Tate is at the other end, doing I don't know what. I wish I didn't care, or have to see him, or notice that he got a cute haircut. I want him to disappear, because that's probably the only way I'll ever be able to stop thinking about him.

"Why didn't you text me back?" he asks, like *he's* annoyed at *me*.

"When?" I ask, because I want to make sure I didn't miss an apology text.

"Um. Last week. I asked you about the periodic table and you never said anything."

I push the cloudy goggles out of my eyes and onto the top of my head. The sun is shining through the window, straight at me. "Oh, maybe you didn't hear. Robo-Beasts don't text." I don't look away. I can feel my heart beating all over my body.

"Okaaay." He drags the word out, stretching it in the air like a piece of bubblegum. Then he looks down and stares into his notebook. He doodles on the lined paper, drawing the same design, his initials, over and over. It makes me feel like I've done something wrong when I haven't. "I don't get why you're being like that," he says.

"You hurt me." I say it like it's obvious, because it should be. "You didn't stand up for me with Kyle. So I don't want to act like everything is fine or talk to you unless I have to. Like right now. For example." I'm looking at him and he's staring at his notebook. He doesn't say anything. I slide my goggles down, cover my eyes, and go back to working on the lab. And even though it's really scary to stand up for myself and have all of my feelings floating around on the outside, it mostly feels good to say what I've been thinking out loud, because I don't want to pretend everything is the same as it was before the dance, when it's not.

twenty-eight

LATE SATURDAY MORNING, I'm sitting at the kitchen counter doing homework, waiting for Mom to wake up. She's supposed to be in bed all the time now, because the baby keeps trying to come out early and he's not done cooking, but she's allowed to get up for food, so I know that eventually she'll make an appearance in the kitchen. I've been thinking a lot about what happened at the hospital and how there was no way Mom would have known what I needed with Dr. Paul if I hadn't told her how I was feeling. I've also been thinking about all the other things she probably doesn't know that I want to tell her now. I think Frannie was right when she said not talking makes everything worse.

It's been pretty quiet around here. Dad has been working even more than usual. According to Mom, he's planning to take a few days off after the baby is born. Normally Dad canceling work for someone else, even someone who's in our family, would cause steam to shoot out of my ears, but I asked him if he did the same thing when I was born, and he did, so it's only fair.

Mom walks into the kitchen. Her blonde hair is sticking up in every direction, and there are deep pillow lines across her face. She takes a fork out of the drawer and opens the fridge, like if she doesn't get something to eat right away, she'll die.

Before I have a chance to say good morning, she's taking a big bite out of a cold meatball. It's weird to see her let go. She's usually so controlled about everything she does. "These are amazing," she says, before she's done chewing. "Have you tried them?"

"I've had them before," I say, trying not to laugh. The baby isn't due for another month, but people have already started sending over food now that Mom is on bed rest: lasagnas, casseroles, and every kind of bread—banana chocolate chip, cranberry, lemon poppy, and long baguettes. Hazel's mom sent her famous sweet cheese kugel topped with Frosted Flakes, and Frannie's dad made the meatballs from scratch. I was surprised they sent anything, since we aren't talking, but maybe their parents don't know that. I wonder who told them about Mom. I wish I had.

She takes the pot of meatballs out of the fridge and sits down on a stool next to me. "Can you help me with some of this food? And also carry all the dishes into my room?" She smiles at me. "I need to go lie down again, but I'm starving."

"Yes and yes." I grin. "It's official. We're having a picnic!"

I take containers out of the fridge, stack them up, and carry them into Mom's room. She's lying on the chair by the TV with her feet up.

"Thank you so much, honey," she says as I spread a blanket out on the floor and put down the food.

"You're welcome," I say and sit down in front of the containers. "What would you like first?"

"Kugel, please."

"You're going to eat the rest of it, aren't you?"

"Maybe." She looks up at the ceiling like she's guilty. "But I promise to save you a corner piece."

"Deal." I uncover the foil and hand her the tray and a clean fork. Then I dig into the lemon pound cake.

"Hey, Mom, the other day at the hospital—thanks for kicking the doctors out and holding my gown and telling Dr. Paul to talk to me. I'm really glad I told you everything. It helped a lot."

"That's all I want to do. I'm sorry if I've made this harder on you." She sighs. "It's not easy for me to be there. That's where I got my brace and had my surgeries. I felt so trapped as a patient, and helpless. It's not any different as a parent. But I haven't been there for you all the time, and that's not fair. I want you to tell me what you need so I can do a better job supporting you from now on."

I nod. "I actually have something else to tell you." I take a deep breath. "I don't like it when you talk about how much harder everything was for you. I mean, I know my brace is nothing compared to surgery. And I'm used to having a brace now, but it's still hard sometimes."

"I was trying to make you feel better." Mom gives me a look like she's waiting for me to figure out that she's right.

"How would knowing you had an even harder time ever make me feel better?"

"I thought it would help if you knew it could be worse," she says. "Don't you think I know how hard this is for you? I wish this wasn't happening. I wish there were something I could do to make your scoliosis go away," she says, like she's trying to push back tears. "I don't blame you for hating me. It's my fault the treatment is so strict and that they're monitoring you so closely. It's because of your family history—my history."

"I don't hate you." I shake my head. It surprises me how wrong Mom is about how I feel. She couldn't be more off.

"You don't?" She sounds confused.

"No. I don't. It's not like you wanted me to have scoliosis," I say. "I just want you to understand that having a brace is hard for me, even if it's not as hard as surgery."

She nods. "I do. I felt just like you. I wanted to be regular. Normal. Whatever that means." She rolls her eyes. "I wasn't. Ever. I felt like such a freak. My brace covered my breasts. It made me look like a cardboard box. And I felt like everyone knew there was something wrong with me. My God. It's so hard to talk about it. To even think about it." Mom is crying. She shakes her head. "Does that help? To know your mother was a total freak?"

"It helps a lot," I say.

Mom is looking at me like I have three heads. "I never told you how I felt, because I didn't want you to think those things about yourself."

"I like knowing I'm not the only one who's ever felt this way," I say. "Maybe it's weird, but it makes me feel like *less* of a freak."

"It's not weird." She shakes her head. "It makes a lot of sense, actually. I had no idea I was upsetting you so much. I wasn't doing it on purpose."

"I know," I say, because I'm sure that's true. I stand up and put my arms all the way around Mom, hugging her and the baby.

"You're so strong. Do you know that?" Mom takes my hands in hers and squeezes them tight. "You've had to be."

I nod at her and smile. I know it's true. I can handle more now, because of everything I've been through with my brace.

"I was thinking that if you want to have friends over tonight, you're more than welcome to," she says. "Really, Rachel. I know you're trying to be considerate, and it's very sweet, but I don't want you to stop everything for me. We have a while longer before the baby comes."

“I don’t have anyone to invite over,” I say.

“Oh, honey.” Mom covers her mouth. “You haven’t made up with the girls.” She looks at me like she knows how much it hurts.

“I would have stood up for Hazel,” I say. Thinking about it makes tears stream down my cheeks. I don’t bother to wipe them away.

“I know you would have.” Mom sighs. “I’m sorry.”

“Thanks.” I shrug.

“You know, what happened doesn’t make Hazel a bad friend. She still has things to learn. She probably hasn’t had an experience where someone treated her the way Kyle treated you, so she doesn’t really know what it feels like to be in your position. I think you should talk to her, give her a chance to understand where you’re coming from, like when you told me how you felt going to see Dr. Paul.”

“I never thought about it like that.”

She nods. “I know your brace doesn’t usually feel like a good thing, but wearing it has forced you to deal with being different, and that’s given you a new perspective. It’s actually a pretty big advantage.”

I nod back. “I think you might be right.”

“First time for everything.” Mom smiles, and then starts crying again. “Oh, these stupid hormones.” She wipes her face dry.

We both laugh.

"What's going on in here?" Dad asks, walking into the bedroom in his suit. He just got home from making rounds at the hospital.

"Picnic. Dig in," I say and hand him a fork.

He smiles. "Looks good."

"It is," Mom says.

"Dad, do you think you could come to my next appointment with Dr. Paul?" I ask. "It helped to have you there."

"Oh, sweetheart," Mom says. "I don't think that's possible."

"Hold on a minute," Dad says. "Why don't you let me answer the question?"

"I'm sorry. I just—"

"It's okay," Dad says to Mom. He reaches into the pocket of his suit jacket and pulls out his phone. "What day is it again?"

"February tenth," Mom and I say at the same time.

"Tuesday," he says to himself, scanning everything in front of him.

I hold my breath.

"I'll make it work." He looks at me and then at Mom. "I'll be there. I promise."

"Thank you," I say.

"I'm glad you asked," Dad says.

"Me too," I say.

"Me three," Mom says.

We finish the meatballs, kugel, and half of the lemon pound cake before Mom goes back to bed and Dad starts his billing. I go upstairs to my room to call Frannie and Hazel. Neither of them pick up. I leave long, rambling, nonsense messages that basically say I'm ready to talk. And I'm sorry.

Then I spread out my homework on the kitchen table and stare at my phone, willing it to ring. I put on a playlist and start jamming. I only have two more months left of my brace drum, so I have to make the most of it now while I still can. An hour, half a playlist, three word problems, and no phone calls later, the garage door opens and closes, which is weird because everyone who lives here is home.

When I look up, Hazel and Frannie are standing in front of me. I push myself out of the chair so I'm standing up too.

"I dumped Kyle," Hazel blurts out.

It's the last thing I expect her to say. "Not because of me? You didn't have to do that," I say, and I actually mean it.

She shakes her head. "I don't know what I was thinking. He's really mean," she says. "He says stuff about everyone, even his best friend. Even his girlfriend."

"What did he say about you?" I ask.

"He kept trying to go to second base." Hazel looks around the room like she's afraid her mom or my mom might be standing behind her. "I said no. Not because I'm, um, you know, small. I just didn't want to. I wasn't ready. He said if I didn't do it, he'd break up with me."

"I hate him," I say.

"That's not the worst part," Frannie says. "Kyle told the whole boys' soccer team that Hazel went to second base with him."

"WHAT?" I shout.

"He's such a liar," Hazel says. "I mean, hello, there's nothing to grab!"

I'm not sure if I'm allowed to laugh, but I can't help it. Frannie can't either.

"I'm sorry," Hazel says. "I didn't know what it felt like to have everyone talking about me. I didn't get it at all."

"I'm sorry too. I didn't tell you how I was feeling. I should have."

Hazel runs over and hugs me. I hold on tight and look over at Frannie. "I'm so sorry for what I said to you. It was mean and not true and I know you were trying to help."

"Don't do that again, okay?" she says.

I nod. "I promise."

"Even if we don't get what's going on with you. Don't freeze us out."

"I won't. I swear," I say.

"Wait, one more thing," Hazel says. "I already apologized to Frannie about this, but I'm sorry I told you that Frannie talked about your brace behind your back. She didn't. It never happened. I made it up for dramatic effect."

"It was very effective," I say. "Next time we fight—"

"There won't be a next time." Hazel cuts me off.

"There might be." I shrug.

"But it'll be different," Frannie says.

"Yeah," I say. "Really different."

Hazel and I run over to Frannie and we all hug.

"Not to change the subject to me, but can we please talk about my birthday and what we're doing for it, because it's less than a month away," Frannie says. "And it has to be really good."

"Yes!" Hazel and I both say at the same time.

"Hi, girls." Mom walks into the kitchen.

"Your stomach is huge!" Hazel covers her mouth, like she's trying to push the words back in. "I so did not mean to say that out loud."

"It's true." Mom smiles. "I hope you're hungry. We have a lot of food to get through. I think you should call home. You might have to sleep over."

"Yes!" Hazel shrieks, rushing over to her backpack. Frannie is already calling her dad.

I smile at Mom, and she smiles back.

Frannie and Hazel both fall asleep in the middle of *Girls Just Want to Have Fun*. I can't sleep. I'm hyped up and dizzy from too much sugar and making up with my best friends. I can't stop myself from taking out my phone and texting Tate: I think you should apologize to me.

He writes back almost immediately. I know. I'm really sorry, he says. I shouldn't have gone along with Kyle like that. It wasn't cool.

Why did you? I don't want to guess.

I don't know, he says. I'm an idiot.

Well, as long as you know that, I say.

I do. Kyle and I aren't friends anymore. I don't want to be friends with someone who's so mean. I wanted to tell you that in class, but I didn't know if you cared anymore.

I care, I say. Why were you friends in the first place? No offense.

He doesn't text back right away, and then my phone starts buzzing. Tate is calling me. "Hey," he says. "Can you talk instead? My answer was too long to text."

"Yeah, sure." I keep my voice low, because Frannie and Hazel are sleeping. Then I walk into the hallway so I don't wake them up.

"Cool," he says. "So, Kyle and I started being friends a long time ago. He didn't used to be like that. He changed a lot at the end of last year and then even more this year. I should have stood up for myself when it started happening, but that was right when Adam left for college and I couldn't even get him on the phone. I guess I didn't want to lose anyone else."

He pauses. "And I definitely should have stood up for both of us at the formal, but after Adam didn't show up to the race on Thanksgiving, I guess I just held on to the only real thing I had."

"Kyle?" I ask.

"I know it sounds dumb," he says. "I told Adam everything that happened, and he said I already lost Kyle last year when he stopped acting like a friend. And he was sorry he wasn't there for me when I needed him. But I feel bad that I dragged you into it. I was being such a follower."

"Yeah, you really were," I say.

"I'm sorry," he says. "Do you think you can forgive me?"

I think about his question for a minute. Not because I'm trying to make him wait or anything, but because I want to tell him the truth.

"I think so," I say. "I'm really glad you explained what happened."

"Me too," he says.

I take a deep breath. "So, Frannie and Hazel are actually at my house. I mean, they're asleep in the other room, but they might wake up, so I should probably go back in there."

"Oh, okay, um . . . Have fun."

"Thanks," I say and hang up.

As soon as I'm off the phone and back in the room with my sleeping friends, I get another text from Tate: Anyone up?

Still sleeping, I say.

I just wanted to say I like you, in case you couldn't tell. I mean, I know we kissed, but I wanted to say it, because it meant a lot to me.

It meant a lot to me too, I say.

twenty-nine

WHEN I GET to school on Monday, I go straight to the gym, because that's where Coach Howard said the team lists would be posted. I've been on a roller coaster all morning. One minute, I'm sure I'll make the A Team. How could I not? Then out of nowhere, all I can think about is every step I took that wasn't perfect, every stumble, every weak pass, and how much I want this. More than I've ever wanted anything.

Hazel and Frannie are both waiting by the door when I get to the gym.

"Finally!" Hazel says.

"Well?" I ask.

"Little Miss Superstition over here"—Hazel nods at Frannie—"thought it would be bad luck if we looked without you."

I smile. "Thanks."

"Let's go," Frannie says, pulling us over to the lists.

There's a small group standing in front of the piece of paper taped to the door. I take a deep breath and look up. *Rachel Brooks. Rachel Brooks.* I keep repeating my name in my mind, willing it to be on the A Team.

GIRLS' SOCCER:

A Team

Ladan Saif

Frannie Tucker

Saaya Rao

Hazel Levy

Zeva Joseph

Lauren Armstrong

Katrina Cruz

Josie Mora

Jennifer Fine

Alice Chung

Brianna Smith

Rima Patel

Rachel Brooks

Emily Wilson

Angela Vincent

I did it! I made the A Team! It feels like cold, hard proof that I'm a good soccer player. Even now. Even in my brace.

Frannie and Hazel both hug me, holding on tight. We're squealing and jumping up and down. And it feels so good.

I get to science early. Tate is standing by the door, leaning against the wall in the hallway like he's waiting for me. My stomach flips. It's the first time I've seen him since we texted about our kiss, and now I'm not sure what to expect or what to do with my hands. All I can think about is how stiff and heavy they feel hanging by my side. Maybe they're always like this and I'm only noticing it now because I'm nervous.

"Congrats on making the A Team," he says as soon as he sees me.

He heard! "Thanks." I grin. "I'm so excited!"

"You should be."

"Wait, when is Adam coming home for the holidays?" I ask.

"This weekend. We're going skiing." He smiles. "What about you?"

"Um, nothing. You know, my mom's having a baby in a month."

"Oh yeah, duh," he says. I know the bell is about to ring, because the hallway is crowded with people on the way to first period.

"Ooo, kissy, kissy." I know it's Kyle before I even look over at him. "I hope you're happy with your freak girlfriend, Tate-O, because we're done, bro. No takebacks on this friendship."

“Um, Kyle,” I say. “Everyone knows you guys aren’t friends anymore and Hazel dumped you because you’re a jerk. So figure it out.”

“Whatever, freak,” he shoots back.

I roll my eyes. “Got anything better? That’s getting old.” Kyle doesn’t say anything. “Nothing? Well, you should work on that.” I turn away from him and look back at Tate. He smiles at me and we walk into science together.

thirty

ON FRIDAY, I'M sitting in English when my teacher says I need to go to the office and take my bag, because Dad is waiting for me. That can mean only one thing: My brother is here! I close my notebook as fast as I can and shove it in my bag.

When I get to the office, Dad is pacing. He stops as soon as he sees me. "The baby came a little earlier than we expected."

"That's great!" I say. I'm trying to seem excited, but really I'm worried I won't like him or I won't feel anything. I think that might be worse.

In the car, on the way to the hospital, Dad rolls down the windows. It's warm outside, really warm for December. I'm wearing my black dress and sweating inside my brace. I put on my "Dad Approved" playlist, which is mostly Paul Simon with a little Billy Joel. I tap on my brace and we sing along, letting our voices float out the window all the way to Boston.

"I think we should start a new tradition," Dad says. "Just you and me."

"Like what?" I ask.

"I looked at the Boston Breakers' schedule. If we get season tickets, we'd end up going to a game every other week. I figured we could get sundaes for dinner and then go watch. But I'm not even sure you like pro soccer, so we can think of something else if you don't." He sounds almost nervous.

"I love all soccer!" I say. "But will it be okay with work?"

"Yes. I already took care of that." He looks over at me.

"Are you serious?" I ask.

"So, does that mean you want to go?"

"Yes! It's perfect."

The maternity floor smells like sour milk, but as soon as we walk into the room, it smells like Mom.

"Hi, baby," she says, reaching out for me with her free arm. She's subtly rocking the tiniest bundle I've ever seen in the other. "Sit next to me." She pats the extra space in her hospital bed.

I can't maneuver myself onto the elevated mattress in my brace, so I stand next to her, leaning against the side of the bed, and look at the baby. He's a tiny blob wrapped up in a yellow blanket, a golden raisin with a sweet little face. His eyes are mostly shut, but they move back and forth and around the room, so I know he's in there. I can't stop staring at him.

Mom's eyes are swollen around the edges and underlined

with dark smudges. It looks like at any moment she could fall asleep. "Want to hold him?" she asks.

"Yes," I say and sit down in the chair next to her bed.

Mom hands the peanut to Dad.

"Make sure you hold his neck," he says, putting him in my arms. "His name is Daniel Aaron Brooks. We're going to call him Danny."

"That's one of my names. The names I wanted," I say.

"It was one of my favorites too," Mom says.

Danny starts crying a little. He looks so helpless with his squinty eyes and missing teeth, yelling for attention. I feel like that too sometimes, whenever I can't say what I need. I bounce him a little until he stops and closes his wrinkly eyes again.

"Look at you," Dad says. "You're already a pro."

"Really, Rachel. You're a natural," Mom says.

I look down at him and feel myself smile. I have a little brother.

One of the nurses comes in to check on Mom.

"Would you mind getting a picture of all of us?" Dad asks.

"Of course," she says, taking his phone from him.

I stand up slowly, careful not to topple over or crush the peanut against my brace, and hand him to Mom.

Dad comes around and stands next to me.

"Smile," the nurse says.

And we all do.

thirty-one

THE GOOD THING about Danny coming early is that I get to spend all of winter vacation hanging out with him. Big news: Danny likes me better than everyone else, but only when I'm in my brace. Something about my hard, plastic stomach puts him right to sleep. He's not interested in my regular stomach. I also tried putting him next to the brace when I wasn't wearing it. He hated that too.

"Let's go," Mom says a few days after Christmas, walking into the family room with Dad. "You and I are going out for a girls' coffee, just the two of us. We need to get out of the house."

I'm pretty sure that's code for *she* needs to get out of the house. "Where are we going?" I ask.

"Biscotti's," she says. "You can get whatever you want."

I pull myself up off the couch and hand Danny to Dad. He starts screaming like a banshee, which is pretty much all he does when he's not sleeping. "Good luck with that," I say to Dad.

"Thanks." Dad rocks the baby back and forth, which doesn't do anything. I like being the only one who can make him stop crying. It's like the brace gives me special baby-calming superpowers.

Biscotti's is always packed, but today the line is wrapped all the way around the store.

"Cinnamon chip muffin?" Mom asks me.

"Yes," I say. "Always."

"Rachel, hey." Tate is walking over to me, fiddling with the zipper on his hoodie.

I can't help but smile. We've been texting and talking a lot over winter break. It's been flirty and also sort of serious—like before the dance, but better.

"I'll be a while," Mom whispers in my ear, and then she walks away.

"Aren't you supposed to be skiing with Adam right now?" I ask Tate.

"Yeah. We're leaving soon. We were up way too late playing video games," he says and grins. "Did I tell you he's home until the end of January? That's how college works. No school for half of December and all of January."

"That's so not fair," I say. "I want to be in college."

"I know, right? But it's pretty great for me." He pauses. "You look different. Good different," he adds quickly.

"Yeah?" I look down at myself. I'm in my brace and my favorite, most comfortable sweats. No lip gloss. No cover-up. My hair is pulled back in a low ponytail. I look the way I always do when I'm doing homework or hanging out at home, like my regular self. I smile, because I sort of like this version of me the best. "Thanks," I say.

"How's the new little bro doing?" he asks. "Still crying a lot?"

"I'm not trying to brag, but he's sort of obsessed with me. Mostly with my brace." I tell him about my superpowers. It's weird how talking about the brace doesn't feel bad anymore or like something that's embarrassing. It feels neutral, like white or water or Switzerland. Or maybe it's even better than that—natural, like me without lip gloss.

"That's awesome," he says. "What's it like to have him around all the time?"

"He mostly cries and sleeps." I don't say "poops," even though that is another thing he does, because no. Just no.

"I've never held a baby before," he says. "I bet it's cool."

"Yeah. It really is," I say.

"Hey—Rachel." Tate looks down at the floor, then back up at me. His hands are shaking. "I was wondering if . . ." He stops himself and puts his hands in his pockets. "Do you, um, want to go out with me?"

"Yes!" I say and smile so big.

He smiles and takes a deep breath, letting out all the air.

Then I hug him right in the middle of Biscotti's, where everyone can see. And he hugs me back.

thirty-two

TODAY IS JANUARY 5, aka Frannie's birthday. It's not a regular birthday. She's thirteen, which I personally think sounds so much older and cooler than twelve. It's a different league. She's officially a teenager. Also, today happens to be our very first A Team practice, and it's a costume practice. How Frannie is that? It feels like fate.

It's one of those weird weather days where it's warmer than it should be outside, but the heat is still blasting in all the school buildings. I'm sticky and sweating. I'm also nervous for practice, and not exactly jumping for joy about adding a costume on top of my normal soccer stuff on top of my brace. I can't wait for February 10.

After school, Hazel and Frannie sort through bags of denim accessories and cowboy hats in the locker room. Frannie picked the Wild West as our theme. "Thank God you're here," she huffs as soon as she sees me, like I'm late, when I'm not.

"Where have you been? With your boyfriend?" Hazel drags out the word.

"Um, no," I say, but I'm blushing anyway. "I was with Coach Howard. I wanted to make sure we could put on the special Frannie playlist during warm-ups today."

"Thank you!" Frannie shrieks.

"Happy birthday!" I hand her a bag of red-and-white-checkered bandannas.

"I love them so much!" She hugs me before I can stop her. "Why are you soaked?"

"It's a sauna inside this thing," I say.

"Gross," she says.

"Tell me about it." I don't feel like faking anything. "I'm sorry, but dressing up is really stressing me out right now. I'm already freaking out about being the worst person on the A Team and sharing the gym with the boys, and on top of that every single person who shows up today will be wearing some cute little outfit, like you guys, and I'll be the only gross, sweaty blob." I stop talking to come up for air.

"Sweaty blob?" Hazel laughs, and soon she's laughing too hard to talk. So is Frannie. I can't help but laugh too.

"I'll only wear what you can," Frannie says.

"That's stupid. You don't have to do that," I say.

"We want to," Hazel says.

"Okay. But—"

"No." Frannie shakes her head, serious again. "I had no clue. About any of that."

"Me neither," Hazel says. "Ugh. I'm so sorry about the sauna situation. That must be really hard."

"Thanks." I smile, because right now it actually feels okay.

Frannie clears her throat. "Now we need to finish getting ready."

We decide on hats, these really thin dark brown vests that won't show how much I'm sweating, and bandannas around our necks. And Hazel asks Coach Howard if she can turn the heat down in the gym, which helps a lot.

Even though it's a school night, we're allowed to have a sleepover for Frannie's birthday. The three of us camp out in her basement with takeout and *Footloose*.

We're halfway through the movie when I say, "I might be getting my brace off in five weeks and one day." I wasn't planning on telling Hazel and Frannie—I figured it'd be better to wait until I got the official word—but I'm feeling so good, I couldn't hold it in any longer.

"What?" Hazel screams. "Are you even serious right now?"

"Yeah." I nod. "I'm almost done growing. And that's what we've been waiting for, so yeah."

“That’s amazing,” Frannie says, pausing the movie. I guess my news is big enough to stop everything.

“Seriously!” Hazel says. “Are you dying right now? You have to be. I mean, this is huge. We need to plan something really big to celebrate!”

I smile. It feels good to have them get excited for me. It makes it seem more real, like maybe I can start to imagine what it will be like when it’s all over. “I’m pretty sure these are going to be the longest five weeks and one day of my life,” I say.

“Yeah. Probably.” Frannie nods.

“I’m a little scared too.” I don’t know where the words come from. “I mean, I want to be done with the brace more than anything. I want it to be over forever. I never want to think about it again. . . . But in a weird way, I am kind of used to it?”

“That makes sense,” Frannie says.

“What makes you nervous?” Hazel asks.

“I know how to be a person with a back brace now, and pretty soon I’m going to be a person without one again,” I say. “It’s going to be different.”

“I’d be nervous about that too,” Hazel says. “It’s like you’re excited. But not just excited.”

I nod. I guess change is pretty scary. Even if it’s the good kind.

thirty-three

THE HOUSE IS quiet for the first time in weeks. The peanut isn't crying, so he must be sleeping. "Hi, honeys," Mom whispers, walking into the kitchen.

"Hi," I say, looking up from my book.

"Hi," Dad says, looking up from his billing.

"I wanted to remind you that we have our appointment with Dr. Paul next week." Mom rests her hands lightly on my shoulders.

"Okay," I say. "Thanks." Even though I've been counting down, waiting for this moment, it feels good that Mom is telling me in advance.

"Is there anything else you need before we go?" she asks.

I shake my head.

Seven days later, Dr. Paul pulls up the x-rays of my spine on the monitor. Then he opens the image of my wrist. This is the one that tells my fate. The growth plates will show if I'm done, if I'm free.

Nothing is guaranteed. I know that. I shouldn't be thinking about going to practice today without my brace, but I am.

The room is silent. Even the flock of doctors is quiet. Dad is facing Dr. Paul, but his eyes are shifting back and forth between the two images. When the creases in his forehead unfold, I know he's done concentrating. He knows the answer.

Mom is staring at the ground, gripping the sides of her chair. Danny is sleeping in his stroller, covered in cotton blankets. He hasn't made a peep since we got to the hospital. I wonder if he can tell how nervous we are. It seems like he's trying to be calm for all of us.

I look back at Dad. I wish he'd be the one to tell me, but that isn't happening. I close my eyes and wait for Dr. Paul to deliver the news.

The tiny room is hot between the lights and the doctors.

Dr. Paul clears his throat, and I almost jump out of my seat. "She's finished growing."

He says it in this nonchalant way, so I'm not sure if I've heard him right. I look at Mom and Dad in case I imagined it. Dad slaps his hand against his leg. He does that whenever he hears good news. They're both smiling, big ones that stretch all the way across their faces. Dad's eyes are even glossy, like he could cry, or maybe he *is* crying. I've never seen it before, so I'm not really sure what I'm looking for. I guess I knew the brace was hard on him, because it's been hard on Mom and on me, but it never occurred to me that Dad wants what I want, for me to be okay and for this to be over.

Then Dr. Paul sighs. "David," he says, looking at Dad. "I really think—" He pauses, shifting his weight, like he's not sure what to say or if he should say whatever is about to come out. I'm already thinking about calling Hazel and Frannie and how I'm going to actually say it to them: "Hey guys, I have news." Or: "Fran. Hazel. I'm out. Done. I'm free."

"Rachel is done growing," Dr. Paul says. "But as a precaution, I'd like to keep her in the brace for another six months."

What? I can't breathe. My lungs feel like they're shutting down. He said I had to wear the brace until I was done growing, and I'm done. Everyone said that. It's not fair. I feel the tears coming, building behind my eyes.

Dr. Paul shuts off the screen, like the decision has been made, like it's final. There's no room for discussion. He's a dictator. "We'll schedule another appointment three months from now and go from there," he says.

"No," Mom says. "No."

"Amy." Dad says her name like she's in trouble.

"No. It's not fair. It's not okay. She should be getting out of the brace today." Mom sounds like she's out of breath. "Rachel did exactly what we asked her to do, and now we're changing the rules."

"We're doing what's best for her spine in the long run," Dr. Paul says.

"But what about what's best for the rest of her?" Mom asks.

"It's six months," Dr. Paul says, like he has a clue what that means, when he doesn't. He doesn't have to wear it.

I look down at my brace by my feet. It's stained on the inside with sweat and yellowed like a trophy. The thick padding under the plastic is worn from rubbing against my body. Even though it's on the ground, I can still feel it around me, squeezing me. I think about how good it would feel to chuck it in the trash with the hazardous waste and toxic materials and never think about it again.

I'm ready to be done. Forever. I want it to be over. But I have this feeling that it's not that easy, and that the brace will still be there even when it's not. It's part of me now, in this way that I can't erase or throw away, and maybe I don't really want to.

I look at Dad. "What will happen if I stop wearing it now?" I ask.

He looks at Dr. Paul. "I'm not sure. You're done growing, so most likely the curve won't move very much. That's why Dr. Paul called it a precaution." Then he looks back at me. "I really wish it were different, but Dr. Paul's recommendation is that you stay in the brace."

"I'm sorry, but I'm not wearing the brace for another six months just because Dr. Paul says so," I say. "It's hard. Every day. And some things get easier, but it never stops being hard. If you tell me I'm taking a risk with my health or my posture, I'll wear it for as long as I need to. I'll handle it." I look at Mom. "I can handle anything." As soon as I say it, I know it's true. "But you have to explain it to me. Give me a real answer."

Dr. Paul nods, so I know he's heard me. "There isn't one definitive answer," he says. "Your growth plates in your hands are closed, and you haven't grown any taller in two visits. These are the most reliable pieces of information we have to determine if you are done growing. But it's certainly not conclusive. What I can tell you is that if you stay in the brace for another six months, you will be doing everything you can to eliminate the risk of your curvature progressing. What I'd like to do is have you continue to wear your brace for twenty-three hours a day until our next appointment, and at that point, we can start to wean you out of the brace by gradually reducing your hours."

"Okay," I say. "I'll do it."

"Are you sure?" Mom asks me.

I look right into her eyes when I say it. "Yes. I'm sure."

She nods. And even though her mouth is closed, I can tell she's smiling.

Once the doctors clear out, Mom adjusts Danny's blankets, and I put on the brace.

"I'm sorry the news wasn't what you wanted to hear," Dad tells me.

I shake my head, because even though I love him for saying that, right now I don't need him to be sorry for me. "I'm lucky you were here. Both of you." I look at Mom and then down at Danny. "All of you."

"I can't wait to come back here in six months," Mom says. "I'm ready to be done with this for good."

She's not back to her old self, and neither am I. I hardly remember who that person is anymore, and even if I did, I wouldn't want to be her. She's gone, and so is the old Mom and the old Dad and our family before Danny. Everything is new and better and stronger. Especially me.

Author's Note

Scoliosis is an abnormal curvature of the spine that affects an estimated seven million people in the United States. While girls are eight times more likely than boys to need treatment, this condition affects children of all genders, races, and social classes. Scoliosis impacts children with congenital and neuromuscular diseases, but it is most common in healthy children, where it usually has no known cause.

I was one of those kids, and at eleven, I got a back brace for scoliosis. The "S" curve in my spine had progressed to twenty-five degrees, and my doctor wanted to do everything possible to avoid surgery, which my mom had undergone when she was my same age. He prescribed a Boston back brace, similar to the brace Rachel wears in this book, for twenty-three hours a day until I was done growing. It hurt to breathe and move inside my thick plastic shell, and everything was harder—standing, sitting, sleeping, getting dressed, having friends, and just being a kid. I felt confined by my new responsibility and closed off from my friends.

Over time my brace became easier to manage physically, but emotionally I never adjusted. During the two years and four months I spent in a brace, I didn't open up to anyone about how alone and insecure I felt. I held my pain inside. It took all of my strength to go to school acting like nothing had changed, while at the same time feeling uncomfortable and exposed. I used my brace as a shield, because I didn't want anyone to see me the way I saw myself—as different. As an adult, I can see that was a mistake. I never stopped hating my brace, and it was such a big part of who I was every day that it had a negative effect on my self-image. I struggled for a long time after my brace came off to break that pattern of insecurity.

It wasn't until I was in my twenties, when I started talking about my experience of being treated for scoliosis, that I realized how alone I'd felt. Since I began working on Rachel's story, I have met many people with scoliosis, including my editor. I've found that connecting with others who went through a similar experience has allowed me to feel understood and see the incredible impact wearing a brace had on my life. It has also made me aware and more sensitive to the fact that many of the people around me felt different in some way as kids. My hope is that by raising awareness about and sensitivity for kids with scoliosis, Rachel's story might be a gateway to heightened understanding for others. I know now that had I let even one other person in on my pain, I would have felt less alone, and maybe instead of feeling different, I would have been able to see that I was strong and fearless and most of all brave.

Listed here are places where you can connect with other kids being treated for scoliosis and read more about the condition and how it gets treated:

Curvy Girls Foundation, Inc.
www.curvygirlsscoliosis.com

Scoliosis Research Society
www.srs.org

National Scoliosis Foundation
www.scoliosis.org

Acknowledgments

This book would not exist without my amazing agent, Kate McKean. Thank you for being my champion from the very beginning and for holding my hand every step of the way.

I am so grateful to Cheryl Klein, the most incredible editor. Thank you for taking a chance on me, for believing in Rachel, and for sharing pieces of your own scoliosis story in your brilliant, insightful, and always kind editorial letters. This book has come so far from where it started thanks to you. You have taught me so much.

There are a lot of people at Arthur A. Levine Books and Scholastic that helped to make *Braced* a real book. Special thanks to Elizabeth Parisi for designing the most beautiful cover and for sharing your perspective with me, and to Rebekah Wallin, Weslie Turner, and Milena Giunco.

I can't imagine my world without the constant encouragement and support of my author friends and readers—Amy Ewing, Caela Carter, Corey Haydu, Jess Verdi, Mary

Thompson, Mindy Raf, Alison Cherry, and Lindsay Ribar—or where I would be without my teachers and classmates from the New School, especially David Levithan, Susan Van Metre, Caron Levis, and Sarah Ketchersid. I am grateful to Susan Shapiro for telling me I could write a book, and to Erasmo Guerra, Sarah Showfety, Victoria Grantham, Royal Young, and Joe Antol for giving me the strength to try. There are countless teachers who believed in me along the way. I think of you more than you will ever know, but Mrs. Alsop made me believe in myself and taught me I could do anything. Thank you for seeing my strengths and showing me what was possible.

I am very lucky to have a group of forever friends cheering me on. Thank you for listening and for making me laugh: Meredith Sondler-Bazar, Laine Alexandra, Jaimie Mayer, Rachelle Borer, Laura Becker, Emily McGinnis, Hannah Goldstein, Ted Malawer, Rebecca Mansell, Dana Roth, Corey Greene, Robyn Gerber, Nikki Gerber, Elise Dowell, Heather Jameson-Lyons, Billy Lindmark, Pedram Saif, and Stephanie Tankel.

I am grateful to the orthopedic and orthotics teams at Boston Children's Hospital for monitoring, bracing, and taking care of me, especially Dr. John Hall.

I am lucky to have a strong, supportive family. Thank you to my siblings, Caroline and Adam, for everything, but especially for getting me. Papa and Gammie, there are no words to describe how special you are to me. And Bubbe, you are always with me. I miss you.

Dad, thank you for making me feel important and taken care of and for teaching me what it means to work hard. You are an incredible role model and a hero to so many people, especially me.

I wrote this book for every kid who has ever had to be strong, including my mom, the strongest person I've ever known. Thank you for never letting a spinal fusion or a back brace or anything you've been through stand in your way. I learned to never give up from watching you, and it has been a gift.

Andy, you made this (and everything) possible. Thank you for believing in me when I couldn't believe in myself and for loving all of me, especially the part that is still in the brace. I love you.

Don't miss Alyson's next novel, *Focused*!

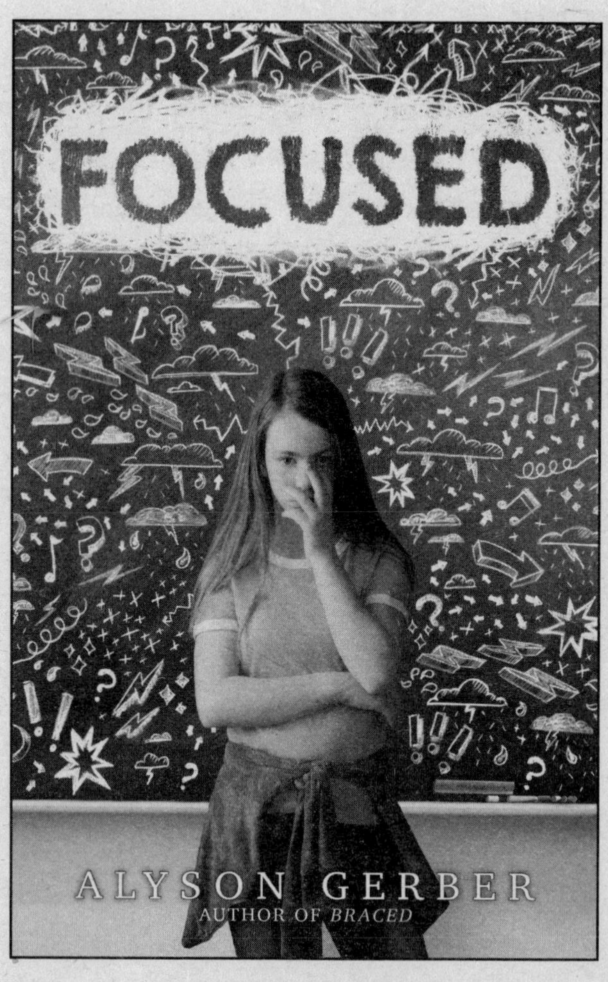

About the Author

ALYSON GERBER wore a back brace for scoliosis from the ages of eleven to thirteen, an experience that led directly to *Braced*, her first novel. She received her MFA in Writing for Children and Young Adults from the New School, and before that she taught elementary and middle school students in a supplementary education program. She lives with her husband in Brooklyn, New York. Please visit her on the web at alysongerber.com and at @alysongerber.